THE OLDEST FEAR
THE OLDEST SIN
AND A BIZARRE MOTIVE FOR MURDER

"I'm a nympho," Beverly explained as she put her hand on my thigh. "Do you find me attractive?"

"Sure," I nodded.

As she unbuttoned her white shirt and took it off, she asked, "Does that excite you or scare hell out of you?"

I just couldn't answer.

She tugged at her shorts. "Why don't we find out?"

Other SIGNET Titles by Carter Brown

- [ ] THE ASEPTIC MURDER (#T4961—75¢)
- [ ] THE BLONDE (#T4883—75¢)
- [ ] BLONDE ON THE ROCKS (#T4682—75¢)
- [ ] THE BODY (#T4550—75¢)
- [ ] BURDEN OF GUILT (#P4219—60¢)
- [ ] CHARLIE SENT ME (#T4775—75¢)
- [ ] THE COFFIN BIRD (#P4394—60¢)
- [ ] THE COVEN (#T4581—75¢)
- [ ] THE CREATIVE MURDERS (#T4520—75¢)
- [ ] A GOOD YEAR FOR DWARFS? (#P4320—60¢)
- [ ] THE INVISIBLE FLAMINI (#T4854—75¢)
- [ ] THE LADY IS TRANSPARENT (#P4344—60¢)
- [ ] MURDER IN THE FAMILY WAY (#T4722—75¢)
- [ ] MURDER IS SO NOSTALGIC (#T5064—75¢)
- [ ] A MURDERER AMONG US (#P4081—60¢)
- [ ] NYMPH TO THE SLAUGHTER (#T4615—75¢)
- [ ] THE PASSIONATE PAGAN (#T4489—75¢)
- [ ] PLAY NOW . . . KILL LATER (#T5013—75¢)
- [ ] THE SAD-EYED SEDUCTRESS (#P4246—60¢)
- [ ] THE SAVAGE SALOME (#T4423—75¢)
- [ ] THE SEX CLINIC (#T4658—75¢)
- [ ] TRUE SON OF THE BEAST (#P4268—60¢)
- [ ] THE UNORTHODOX CORPSE (#P4197—60¢)
- [ ] WHERE DID CHARITY GO? (#T4455—75¢)
- [ ] THE WIND-UP DOLL (#T4826—75¢)
- [ ] W.H.O.R.E.! (#T4798—75¢)

THE NEW AMERICAN LIBRARY, INC.,
P.O. Box 999, Bergenfield, New Jersey 07621

Please send me the SIGNET BOOKS I have checked above. I am enclosing $_____(check or money order—no currency or C.O.D.'s). Please include the list price plus 15¢ a copy to cover handling and mailing costs. (Prices and numbers are subject to change without notice.)

Name_____

Address_____

City_____State_____Zip Code_____

Allow at least 3 weeks for delivery

Carter Brown

DIE ANYTIME, AFTER TUESDAY!

A SIGNET BOOK from
NEW AMERICAN LIBRARY
TIMES MIRROR
in association with Horwitz Publications

© COPYRIGHT 1969 BY HORWITZ PUBLICATIONS, INC.
PTY. LTD., SYDNEY, AUSTRALIA

Reproduction in part or in whole in any language expressly forbidden in any part of the world without the written consent of Horwitz Publications.

All rights reserved

Published by arrangement with Alan G. Yates

THIRD PRINTING

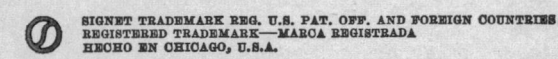

SIGNET TRADEMARK REG. U.S. PAT. OFF. AND FOREIGN COUNTRIES
REGISTERED TRADEMARK—MARCA REGISTRADA
HECHO EN CHICAGO, U.S.A.

SIGNET, SIGNET CLASSICS, SIGNETTE, MENTOR AND PLUME BOOKS
are published by The New American Library, Inc.,
1301 Avenue of the Americas, New York, New York 10019

FIRST PRINTING, JUNE, 1969

PRINTED IN THE UNITED STATES OF AMERICA

CHAPTER ONE

Most dames in Hollywood have more bust than brains. You don't have to be in the business long to wake up to that. The dreamy-eyed hopefuls drift in from as far away as Outer Mongolia. They flock to this honey pot of mass culture that supplies the world with stickum and goo like Mongoloid bees without a hive of their own.

And that's how it is, usually. They're either lost and lonely orphans, full of the ambition to make themselves into something, or they're Midwest beauty queens (Miss Kansas Wheat of 1969) from families so respectable they're dying of boredom. Either way, they're ripe fruit on the tree, ready for the calloused hands of the flesh pickers in Hollywood's multimillion dollar canneries. They're after the excitement, the thrills, the fun, the fame, these bright-eyed beautiful girls without enough moxie between them to fill a walnut shell.

Mostly, they get picked, sucked dry, and thrown out in a heap with the other discards. The experience wises up a few of them, but the majority end up hard and bitter beneath their sagging exteriors of glamorous have-beens. These, the ones who have been taken for a short ride by the big and the smart, spend the rest of their lives taking it out on the small and stupid. That's what makes this world profitable for guys like me to work in. Everyone has a grudge, and a lot of people are on the lookout for someone to take it out on. In Hollywood, they beat the national average all to hell.

A few of the best make it to the top. Some have the

luck, some have the drive, some make the right connections with the ruthless single-mindedness everyone professes to admire. Some, of course, have the talent.

It isn't the bright ones who deliver my daily bread. Not usually. I usually see the ones who need a friendly father to explain a fake fairyland to a mixed-up sexpot. But there are exceptions.

Sonia Mayer was a beautiful example of the exception who makes you wonder about the rule. She was close to thirty, I guessed; a blonde, with her hair swept up from just above her left ear, then across the top of her head until it plunged in a swirling cascade all the way down to her right shoulder. A tiny copper bell—dangling at the bottom of a long pendant that hung from the naked earlobe—tinkled faintly when she moved her head. Her eyes were gray-green, wide and knowing; her nose was short and straight, and her full lips had a curving arrogance all their own.

She was wearing a beige silk dress with a neckline scooped low enough to reveal four inches of deep cleavage. The whole deal was supported by a couple of slender straps that just didn't look equipped to handle any sudden deep sigh. In a world rapidly becoming overpopulated with flat-chested neuters—so beloved by the illegitimate priests of high fashion—her figure was refreshingly out of style. Her hips were amply rounded to match the delicate taper of rounded calves and neat ankles. Whenever she moved her head I could hear that tinkling little copper bell calling to me.

"How come a beautiful blonde like you happens to be the personal manager of a comic like Sam Sorel?" I asked.

"I cut my teeth in one of the big talent agencies, Rick." Her voice was a smooth, completely self-possessed contralto. "They let me handle a few of their lesser clients, the ones they were sure would never make it. Then, around two years back, they offered me Sam. He was on the skids and going down fast. They were hoping, of course, that he'd be so insulted by the idea he'd quit the agency. But from the first time we met we took a shine to each other, and it ended up with the both of us quitting the agency."

"You've done one hell of a job," I said respectfully, "putting him right back on top. It couldn't have been easy."

She shrugged her creamy-white shoulders. "Sam always had the talent. He just had to find the faith in himself again."

Nobody in their right mind could doubt Sam Sorel was still the top stand-up comic in the business. The large audience stacked in the exclusive club listened avidly, carefully suppressing their laughter so as not to miss anything. He devoted the last ten minutes of his act to a surrealistic word fantasy of psychoanalysis, which culminated in the analyst advising him to take a long trip for his health's sake, then charging him an extra fifty bucks for the LSD. After the applause had finally died down and the band started in on a new set, you could sense the feeling of relief now that everyone could relax from the concentration demanded by the comic's staccato delivery. Every word was delivered with machine-gun precision and never one wasted.

"We'll give him five minutes before we go around to his dressing room, Rick," Sonia said.

"Why doesn't he join us here at the table and have a drink?" I suggested.

"Not Sam." She smiled, showing strong white teeth. "The only time he can tolerate a crowd is when it's out front of him, beating its collective palms together in appreciation of his comic genius." The copper bell tinkled as she checked her watch. "I think it's time you talked with him."

"You still don't want to tell me anything about his problem first?"

"It's Sam's problem; I think he should tell it." She got up onto her feet. "Now that he's back in Hollywood who else could he take his problem to except Rick Holman?"

It was a compliment that effectively closed off any further discussion. I followed the beige silk bounce of her high-riding bottom, and it kept me entranced all the way to the dressing room. It had been a hell of a long time since I had met a woman with so much sex appeal as Sonia Mayer had. Every moment I was with her I had to fight down a powerful urge to strip off all her clothes and carry her to the nearest couch. There was more to it than the physical desire; she was a completely female-type-female, which added to the compulsive attraction of opposites.

In the dressing room, Sam Sorel was sitting in front of the dresser mirror with a glass in his hand, a half-empty bottle of bourbon at his elbow. He raised the glass in a mock salute as we entered, then drank deeply.

"Sam," the blonde said, "this is Rick Holman."

"Good to see you, Rick." In contrast with the rapid-fire delivery of his act, his speech was now slow and almost hesitant. "Sit down, won't you?"

We took the two straight-backed chairs. Sonia crossed her legs, and one kneecap automatically dimpled, while Sorel took another swig of bourbon before our glances met in the mirror. He had a lean, cadaverous face; the skin was wrinkled and puckered like it had gotten tired of people in spiked shoes running over it the whole time. His eyes were deep-set, a mournful dark brown, and his graying black hair hung lank down over his shirt collar. Somehow he looked like a violin virtuoso with a couple of hundred concerts in back of him who's gotten so goddamned bored with the whole thing he doesn't even listen to himself play anymore.

Waiting for him to get up the courage to face a critical audience, I noticed that the dressing room was larger than the phone booth in the lobby of the club and smaller than the men's room. For a star, it maybe wasn't quite luxurious enough, but I could have gotten that impression because the gold paint on the stucco wall facing the cold, cold outdoors was peeling.

The star himself had his back turned to that wall, and was just downing another bourbon.

"My problem's too big to take to anybody except you, Rick," he said finally. "You're the one with the big rep for discreetly fixing the impossible around Hollywood, and now that I'm back, it's got to be fixed fast."

"We took this three weeks' club engagement just so Sam could keep his hand in," Sonia interrupted in her smooth contralto. "Sam finishes up here tomorrow night, then he starts shooting in a couple of weeks. The motion picture is the important deal."

"Maybe we start shooting in a couple of weeks." Sorel refilled his glass. "It all depends on you, Rick."

"So tell me your problem," I said.

He sighed heavily. "Comics are supposed to be nice people, did you know that? Even sick comics are supposed to spout philosophy because, underneath, their hearts are pure gold. All the rest of the world is supposed to be kind to kids and dumb animals, and love their wives. The professional comic sweats out his heart and guts trying to be funny the whole goddamned time, so there's no time left for anything else. It makes him a heavy drinker, short-circuits his temper, and after a while turns him a little psycho. In the end it's only his audience that's for real. When they switch off the spotlights, all he wants is to be left alone. So he goes home."

"You're breaking my heart," I told him.

"Home is where the wife is." He stared sadly at my reflection in the dresser mirror. "The one thing she's not about to do is leave him alone. She wants money, high-living, attention, vacations, and—most of all—she wants him to listen to *her* troubles. He takes it until he can't take anymore, then ups and leaves both wife and home. But real soon, because he's the loneliest man in the whole goddamned world, he sets up another home with a new wife, then repeats the whole stupid pattern all over again. I've got three ex-wives hanging around my neck, Rick. The alimony payments are big enough to establish a foundation to keep washed-up comics in luxury for the rest of their miserable lives!"

"It sounds more like a problem for your attorneys," I said.

"That's just the background picture, friend," he said, bleakly. "We don't even get to the real problem yet."

"The motion picture, Sam," Sonia prompted.

"Sure," he nodded. "It's been a long haul back to the top and I never would have made it without Sonia." He gave her a quick affectionate glance. "If this picture is right for me—and it sure looks that way—I'll be back on top for a long time. I don't even mind about those alimony payments anymore, just so long as those three bitches leave me alone. But—and right here is my big problem—they won't leave me alone. Leastwise, one of them won't, but I don't know which one out of three it is."

"Getting between a guy and his ex-wives is not my line of business," I told him.

"The hell it isn't!" Sorel exploded. "One of those crazy dames is going to kill me!" He rubbed the back of his hand across one side of his face in a quick, nervous gesture. "I'm not even sure if she's determined to kill me, or maybe she only wants to pull some lousy stunt like a fake try so afterward she can pour her steel-plated heart out to the reporters about Sorel, the bastard who drove her to it. With that kind of publicity, I figure I might as well be dead, anyway."

"Okay," I said reluctantly. "So, I'll listen."

Sonia opened her purse, took out some folded papers and gave them to me. There were three letters; somebody had used the old trick of cutting words out of various newspapers and magazines, then pasting them down onto a sheet of notepaper. The first one read: *Marriage should be forever. I can't live without you, so you are not going to live without me.* The second expanded a little: *You tossed all three of us out like yesterday's garbage, Sam. Now you don't have the time to try and figure out which one of us is going to kill you. I waited until you had gotten back into the big time because it will hurt you more to lose everything now. I am giving you one week to make your final arrangements. You will be dead within the next two weeks.*

The third and final letter started out with a dictionary quote: *Claustrophobia is the morbid fear of confined spaces. That is you, Sam, I remember, and that is how you are going to die—in a confined space. Think about it, because you do not have much time left. I know you cannot run because this stupid movie you will never make means too much to your great ego. Now you have only three days left to make the funeral arrangements.*

You will die one day during the week starting next Tuesday.

"Sam got the first letter about a week back, the second three days ago, and the last one arrived in this morning's mail," Sonia said. "They were all mailed from different sections of Los Angeles."

"It could be somebody's idea of a gag," I suggested.

Sorel shook his head. "Prove it, and I'll love you forever, Rick, but I'm goddamned sure this is no gag. One of those crazy bitches is out to get me!"

"They all live in L.A. and none of them have remarried. Maybe that's some kind of a tribute to Sam as a husband?" Sonia's lips twitched momentarily. "Or maybe the alimony settlements were a little too generous?"

"I'll need names and addresses," I told her.

"I have them already written out for you, right here." She nodded toward her purse which lay on the small table beside her chair. "Sam finishes up this engagement tomorrow night. On Sunday we're moving out of the hotel into a house in Brentwood a friend has loaned us for the next couple of weeks so Sam can relax before he starts shooting. He's not about to relax if he figures one of his ex-wives is going to murder him anytime starting from next Tuesday!"

"That figures," I said generously. "You have any preference for which one of them is about to try and dispose of you, Sam?"

He shrugged massively. "Who knows which one of their tiny barbaric little minds has fractured? If I have to make a guess, I'd go for Beverly. She was always trying to improve my mind the whole goddamned time we were married. But that's still just a lousy guess."

"Suppose we take them in sequence," I suggested. "Who was the first?"

"Linda Galen." His grin was wry and self-deprecating. "She was the girl next door, the one I never did get to meet when I was a kid living out of my old lady's vaudeville trunk. It lasted five years. She was the homey, domestic type, and after the first four years she made everything so goddamned homey I started to suffocate. Then she started to nag; she nagged about everything—my clothes, my friends, my drinking—until I just ran and never did go back." He rotated his glass slowly between his fingers. "She used to knit while she nagged. I'd sit there and listen to those goddamned needles clicking away, and her tongue going even faster, until I'd get this feeling she was knitting me into a cocoon made out of fine steel mesh. Because she wanted me trapped and helpless, wrapped up tight so I couldn't move a finger. Then I'd have no choice but to listen to her goddamned nagging the whole time. I had this picture in the back of my mind of the husk that used to be Sam Sorel rotting away inside the cocoon, while the needles clicked and she ran off at the mouth the whole time, not even realizing I had died six months back!"

"Sam is the one with the imagination," Sonia said lightly. "But that's what gave him a starting-point for his Black Widow routine. It sold one hell of a lot of records."

"Two years a free man, then I got trapped again," Sorel continued in a brooding voice. "My second wife was the intellectual type and the complete opposite of Linda, which figures, I guess. Beverly Quillen was her name and she had a great sense of humor. I should have known that would be fatal from the beginning. She also had a real bitch of a temper. When she got mad she became one of those pot-throwing, screaming harpies. She just couldn't leave my mind alone. I took it for a few months, but then she had the goddamned nerve to start analyzing my act! When it came to the final showdown, she went into the kitchen and came back waving a carving-knife." He held his arm up straight in the air and the coat sleeve dropped back so I could see reflected in the mirror the white scar slashed across his wrist. "After that I knew I'd never sleep nights with her in the same apartment!"

"How long did that marriage last?" I queried.

"A couple of years. Then I hit the skids so fast I was near bottom before I realized I'd even slipped. Too much booze, using the older and easier routines, and—the worst thing of all—building a kind of contempt for my audience. I guess I panicked when the realization caught up with me, Rick. I didn't have any faith in myself anymore, and I needed something to give me a boost real bad. That's when I made the biggest mistake of my whole goddamned life!"

He finished the remains of his drink and quickly refilled the glass. I figured he had gone through around six ounces of straight bourbon in the time I had been inside the dressing room, and if he kept on going at the same rate, he was about to set some kind of alcoholic record.

"Jackie Slater was her name." His voice thickened a little. "A twenty-year-old starlet; a beautifully built slut with a vicious little sewer of a mind! I wanted somebody to believe in me, while she wanted a passport to bigger and better parts at the studios. It took her maybe two months to come to realize she hadn't married Sam Sorel, the top comic, but the 'Who needs him?' Sorel on the skids. So then the rest was just hell on wheels. It finished up with me walking in on her and some beach bum in bed together. She just looked up at me over his shoulder and laughed!"

"So how come you're paying her alimony?" I asked logically.

"Because the goddamned bitch said if I didn't let her divorce me, she'd swear in court the marriage was never consummated. That would have been the biggest laugh I ever got! Can you imagine everybody busting their sides at the thought of Sam Sorel—the funny guy who's so wise about sex and marriage—impotent!" He drank quickly, spilling liquor down the front of his coat. "I tell you, Rick, I almost came to the point of killing her! She was like some filthy leech, clinging to me for all she could goddamned well get out of me! And all the time she was destroying me, and there was nothing I could do about it. I could feel everything draining away—my ability to think, my energy, my manhood—I couldn't even—"

His voice broke suddenly in mid sentence, then his head slumped down between his hands and he began to sob in the noisy, mindless way of a very small child.

There were five long embarrassing seconds before the blonde spoke.

"I guess you have already got enough of the picture for now, Rick?" Sonia asked in a quiet voice.

"Sure," I nodded, then got quickly onto my feet. The harsh sounds of a grown man crying his heart out were beginning to rub my nerve ends the wrong way. "I'll be in touch."

"Thank you." Her voice was still completely self-possessed.

About halfway down the corridor I realized I had forgotten that list of ex-wives and their addresses, so I retraced my steps back to the dressing room. The door wasn't quite closed. I knocked then pushed it wide open.

Sam Sorel was down on his knees beside the blonde's chair. Sonia had her dress pulled down to her waist, the finger-width straps dangling uselessly. She was cradling his head against the bare fullness of her large breasts. Sorel wasn't crying anymore; his eyes were closed tight and there was a look of peaceful contentment on his lined face. For a moment Sonia's eyes met mine, then she nodded toward the purse on the small table beside her chair. I tiptoed across the room—like some stooge that accidentally walks onto the wrong set when they're in the middle of shooting the big scene of the whole movie—took the list from her purse and headed back toward the door.

Sonia Mayer smiled a brief farewell as I reached the doorway, one hand gently pressing Sorel's head even tighter against the deep swell of her breasts. Her gray-green eyes held a look of sure serenity. She looked like Mother Earth incarnate, busy comforting Everyman—who is still only a frightened kid at heart.

The incredible thing was, even though she was naked to the waist, she didn't look sexy at all.

CHAPTER TWO

It was a bright, sunny morning, with the fog lifting fast. I just managed to find a slot for my convertible in the parking lot out front of the modern-looking hotel. There was a convention in progress I realized after passing a half-dozen eager executive-type guys in the lobby, all wearing the identical button proclaiming some electronics outfit was in town. Hell, I wouldn't be surprised if it's an everlasting convention where everybody is doomed to spend eternity whooping it up with a bunch of guys you hate from the home office.

The pillared walk, with the exclusive little shops down one side, was almost empty, and the fountains playing among the cacti still had a kind of new-scrubbed look about them. I found the place I was looking for about halfway down the walk. *Linda's Boutique* was written over the doorway in a chichi fluorescent italic script. Inside, it seemed to offer about everything from an elegant evening gown made from paper, to a micro-mini silk dress that looked more like a blouson top. A very chic brunet around thirty-five appeared from the back of the shop and started toward me with a professional smile of welcome on her face.

"May I help you?" Her voice had a pleasant deep tone.

"I'd like to see the owner," I told her.

"I'm Linda Galen."

"You sure don't look the homey, domesticated type to me," I said truthfully.

15

"How's that again?" Her eyebrows lifted a fraction.

"That's how your ex-husband described you last night," I explained. "Maybe he doesn't see too good?"

Her hair was a lacquered shiny black helmet, which went just fine with the long oval of her face. The dark brown eyes were intelligent and set wide apart; her mouth was nicely curved without being sensual. She was wearing an elegant silk dress consisting of alternate horizontal brown and orange stripes that swirled happily around her full bust, narrow waist, and controlled hips. She looked like she'd be more at home in Acapulco with the jet set than busy in front of some homey kitchen sink.

"Sam?" Her smile lost its professionalism and became genuine. "You know, that's funny! I haven't even thought about him over the last four or five years."

"But you haven't forgotten to pick up the alimony payments each month?"

"Of course not." Her eyes coolly appraised my face. "Are you his attorney, Mr—?"

"Holman, Rick Holman," I said. "I'm the guy who's trying to find out which one of his three ex-wives is threatening to kill him."

"You're a police officer?"

I shook my head. "Sam is right back on top again now. If he took this problem to the police, he wouldn't care for the kind of publicity it would bring him."

"So you're some kind of private detective, Mr. Holman?"

"I guess you could say that," I agreed. "Maybe we could talk about Sam a little? My problem is that whoever wants to kill him probably has good reason, but Sam—naturally—just wouldn't know why anybody would want to kill a nice guy like him."

"It's time I took a coffee break, anyway," she said. "You can pick up the tab on Sam's account, Mr. Holman." She turned her head and called, "Andrea!"

"Yes, honey?" The tall slender blonde who emerged from the back of the shop had long straight hair that hung down below her shoulders, almost far enough to meet the hem of her micro-mini skirt.

"I'm just going out for coffee," the brunet told her. "If you'll mind the store while I'm gone."

The blonde brushed her hair back from her face and stared at the both of us for a long moment while her mouth turned sullen. "Will you be gone long?"

"Maybe twenty minutes." Her boss's voice was very brisk. "I have some business to discuss with Mr. Holman."

A couple of minutes later we were established in the hotel coffee shop. Linda Galen ordered a Danish with her coffee—so maybe those hips didn't need too much control after all?—then settled back in her chair.

"You realize you've just ruined my reputation?" Her voice was obviously meant to sound amused but didn't. "I'm hopelessly compromised now, so far as Andrea is concerned!"

"I guess she has her own problems," I said. "With all that hair hanging down over her face she must be some kind of traffic hazard."

"The mini skirt seems to make her more of a hazard where male drivers are concerned." She shrugged her shoulders, abruptly dismissing the subject. "I keep hearing that phrase in the back of my mind—the homey, domesticated type—just what else did Sam tell you about me?"

"You made everything a little too homey," I quoted. "Then you started to nag him, and you'd knit while you nagged. *Click!* went the needles. *Click!* went your tongue. *Click!* went Sam, finally, out the front door for the last time and never did come back."

"I loved Sam and that's why I married him," she said easily. "But then I found out he didn't want a wife, just a mother. I would have preferred to handle the business side of his career but he wanted the gingham apron bit, complete with bottles of home-preserved fruit in the kitchen. I didn't mind so much the times when he really needed mothering—all those nightmares—but playing Mom to a guy who's thirteen years older than yourself can get to be quite a chore." She smiled faintly. "You know something? Now that I think about it, I

17

did knit and nag at the same time! So I guess he gave you a pretty accurate description of me, after all."

"Nightmares?" I queried.

"He used to get them all the time. Sam had a big complex about being shut-in anyplace. He was always opening windows and doors; he wouldn't fly, he wouldn't even have the windows shut in an air-conditioned car! The nightmares were always the same, apparently, about being buried alive."

The waitress served us, then drifted away. I lit a cigarette and watched Linda Galen tackle her Danish with obvious relish. For sure, she wasn't homey the way Sorel had depicted her, but I doubted if she could be so well adjusted as she made herself out to be. Maybe a little shock therapy might help about here, I figured.

"Can you give me one good reason why you'd want to kill Sam?" I asked.

She thought about it while she finished off the Danish, her face serious with concentration. "Maybe one. It was Sam who killed the idea of marriage for me, forever." She shrugged. "But, who knows? He could have done me a big favor!"

"You've never considered marrying again?"

"Never. This boutique doesn't make me any fortune but it does make a little profit. I get a boot out of running the shop, doing the books, ordering stock, and all." She smiled briefly. "I won't pretend I don't enjoy the alimony, either."

"You'd lose that if you married again?"

"Naturally."

"That makes you a dream-girl for a whole lot of guys," I said coldly. "The rare breed of female who's not interested in seeing the affair end in marriage."

"I don't think I've known you long enough to start a discussion about my sex life, Mr. Holman." Her voice was very casual indeed.

"Do you miss being married to Sorel?"

"Like a hole in the head! But I would miss the alimony because it makes the running of the shop a fun project. So long as that monthly check keeps coming in, I don't have to worry about making a profit." She hesitated for a moment. "There's one question I have to ask you: Are you sure it's one of the ex-wives who's threatening to kill Sam? I mean, I can't imagine the other two wanting to lose their alimony, either."

"Sure," I said, "but since when did logic have anything to do with emotion?"

"Now, there's a profound remark!" Her voice was heavy with sarcasm. "Well, I'm sorry I can't do more to help you find your would-be assassin."

It was obviously meant for a good-bye, and I ignored it. "You said Sam killed the idea of marriage for you forever. Did he also kill the idea of another man for you forever?"

Her eyes were suddenly guarded. "Why do you ask that?"

"You're a very attractive woman, and you must meet a lot of well-heeled guys in a hotel like this. Marriage to one of them would more than compensate for the loss of alimony."

"Thank you for the coffee, and the compliment." She started to get up from the table. "I hope you manage to keep Sam alive for all our sakes. If you'll excuse me, Mr. Holman, I have to get back now."

"Sure." I injected a tone of fake sympathy into my voice. "I do sincerely hope Andrea isn't too jealous when you get back!"

Her eyes beamed bloody murder at me for a moment, then she took off like somebody had just told her the boutique was a mass of flames.

That left me with the tab, and the uncomfortable feeling I had missed a vital point someplace along the line. Anyway, I thought hopefully, there were still two would-be assassins to come. I had a second cup of coffee and another cigarette while I went back over what Linda Galen had told me. The bit about Sorel wanting to be mothered rang true, especially when I remembered the way-out scene I had walked in on the previous night in Sorel's dressing room. What really bugged me was her logical question—Why would any of the ex-wives want to lose their alimony by killing off its source? Five minutes later I was still chewing it over and getting noplace, when a slender blonde swept into the vacant chair opposite me like some kind of miniskirted tornado coming to rest.

"You stinking creep!" She kept her voice down to the kind of whisper that can penetrate a foot-thick concrete wall. "You know what you've done to her?"

"So maybe she's a little mad at me because I recognized the truth?" I said placatingly. "It happens, Andrea."

She pushed the long hair back out of her eyes and glared at me. "I've just left her in the back of the shop having hysterics. If you knew even half the truth about that bastard, Sorel, you wouldn't be trying to save him from getting killed; you'd be out looking for him right now with a shotgun!"

"Why?"

"I guess Linda was too embarrassed to tell you. Well, I'm not!" She took a deep breath but it didn't alter the flat contour of her blouse at all. "Sorel is the kind of egomaniac who just can't stand to let go. Never mind if it was him who finally busted up their marriage, he still figures Linda belongs to him like some piece of personalized property. About three months back he somehow found out about Linda and me." Her mouth tightened. Her eyes dared me to disapprove, and her voice was slightly strained as she spoke. "We have a special kind of relationship. Any comment?"

"None," I told her.

"Fine!" Her black-rimmed eyes sneered at me. "So you do know when to keep your big mouth shut sometimes?"

"You were telling me about the other bastard, Sorel," I reminded her.

"Did he tell you about beating her up?"

"Maybe. But you tell me again."

"He suddenly appeared at Linda's apartment one night around eleven. I think he was drunk; raving like a madman. Said he wasn't going to stand for any ex-wife of his living in an unnatural relationship with another woman, and he used about every filthy word I'd ever heard in my whole life—and a few I'd never heard before! It got to the point where I couldn't stand it any longer, with Linda sobbing her heart out, and all. So I told him to get the hell out of there, and he hit me!"

Her face still registered vague astonishment at the memory. "He just stood there, hauled off, then hit me right in the mouth with his clenched fist. Afterward, while I was still lying half unconscious on the floor, he grabbed hold of Linda and dragged her into the bedroom. I guess I don't have to tell you what happened then? Before he left he told her if she didn't break up her association with me, the next time he visited he'd kill the both of us."

"But you haven't broken up the relationship?"

"Linda moved into my apartment the next day." She couldn't keep the gloating tone of satisfaction entirely out of her voice. "My brother lives right across the hall and he's big enough to take care of two guys like Sorel!"

"He hasn't tried to see Linda again? Not in the boutique or anyplace?" I asked.

She shook her head. "But Linda's still scared he might try, only she won't admit it. You can imagine what kind of reaction you caused with your crazy talk about one of Sorel's ex-wives threatening to kill *him*, then telling her you knew all about us in the next breath!"

"It happened about three months back? Sometime in mid-May, huh?"

"I guess so." She thought for a moment. "It was a Friday night. I remember we were running a sale that week and we couldn't open on Saturday because we were too busy moving Linda into my apartment; it didn't exactly please some of our clients who missed out on the sale. I'm sure it was the second week in May."

"Okay," I said. "Why did you bother coming here to tell me about it?"

"You're working for Sorel," she said in a bleak voice. "I don't know what he's about with this crazy story of one of his ex-wives wanting to kill him, but it could be some devious way of trying to get at Linda again. So I'm giving the both of you fair warning, Holman; leave her alone!"

21

"What's the address of your apartment?"

She hesitated for a couple of seconds, then gave me a West Hollywood address. I checked the typed list Sonia Mayer had given me the night before, and the identical address was there as Linda Galen's home. I wondered about that for a little while, ignoring the blonde's glacial stare.

"Do you want any more information?" she grated. "My full name is Andrea Marco, twenty-two years of age, height five-seven, weight one hundred and five, blue eyes, blond hair, and I mustn't forget the crescent-shaped birthmark on my inner right thigh!"

"You've given me too much information already." I grinned at her nastily. "Like a real good motive for Linda wanting Sorel dead, and I won't forget to add your name to the list of potential killers, either!"

Her mouth dropped open for a moment, then she stiffened. "If I were you, Holman," she said crisply, "I'd start wondering about Sorel's real intentions. Maybe he's figuring on killing one of his ex-wives, like Linda, and he's just using you as some kind of smoke screen."

A moment later she was walking briskly toward the exit, her mini skirt flapping briskly around her upper thighs. Her long shapely legs absorbed the complete attention of every other male inside the room. It didn't seem worth the effort to tell them they were all wasting their time.

CHAPTER THREE

The long drive out to Santa Monica and back didn't impress me with the scenic wonders of Southern California, but it did give me time to think about a few things. If you don't occupy your mind when driving the long miles down Santa Monica Boulevard you die of boredom. Los Angeles is my town, you understand, but they save all the glamour for the back lots.

What I wanted to think about was simple. Did I believe Sam Sorel's story about the notes and his reason for hiring me? And, if I did, what were the chances that the notes were a cover for someone other than his ex-wives?

The trip cost me some gas, but it didn't provide me with any answers.

On the way back I pulled up at a service station next to a phone booth. It cost me ten cents more to talk to Sonia and find out that Sam couldn't be disturbed from his poolside siesta and that, anyway, neither of them could think of anyone at all, in the non-wife category, who could wish Sam dead.

I got back in my car wishing halfheartedly that Sam was dead and I was happily unemployed, and drove away thinking gloomy thoughts about next Wednesday morning.

The motor court where Jackie Slater lived was tucked back one block from Wilshire Boulevard in the borderland between Beverly Hills and Westwood Village. It was two-story white stucco, and it looked expensive. Even the manager's office had wall-to-wall carpet and spare-looking modernistic furniture in teak. I wondered if the pool was lined with mink and they pumped champagne through the filter plant.

A big guy behind the manager's desk got to his feet as I walked into the office. His coarse black hair had been carefully trimmed to allow a short fringe of curls to decorate his forehead. He was wearing a flowered shirt over a pair of tan slacks, and there were hard ridges of muscle bulging under the skin of his bronzed forearms. The blue eyes, set deep in the mahogany-tanned face, gave me a strictly impersonal look.

"I'm Harvey Graham," he said in a courteous bass. "Can I help you?"

"I'm looking for Miss Slater," I told him. "Jackie Slater?"

"She's one of our permanent guests. Number ten, on the far side of the pool. The last time I saw her she was sunbathing out beside the pool, so maybe she's still there." He rubbed his index finger across his lower lip slowly. "No trouble?"

"Just visiting," I said. "Is she expecting trouble?"

"Miss Slater is a professional starlet." He shrugged gently. "With them, there's always trouble."

"You must lead an interesting life," I said mildly.

"Sometimes it gets so I start thinking Pasadena is a swinging sin-city!" He grinned reluctantly. "If you'd been trouble, it would have brightened up my dull morning a little." He flexed his arms so the triceps sprang into startling prominence. "Who knows? Maybe some homicidal maniac will check in after lunch!"

I found Jackie Slater supine on a gaudily striped beach towel close to the edge of the pool. Two small strips of scarlet jersey bikini slashed color contrast across her golden-brown tan. The pneumatic curves and spheres of her incredible body would have made a stunning foldout for a new men's magazine called *Lust*. A tangle of tight silver-blond curls surmounted the Kewpie-doll face, and the white lip salve smeared heavily across her mouth gave her a bizarre look. Huge blue-framed sunglasses hid her eyes, so I couldn't tell if she was asleep or just thinking.

"Miss Slater?" I asked.

"Get lost!" Her voice was hoarse and unlovely.

"I'm from Central Casting," I said seriously. "Stellar Productions is doing a remake of *Rain*, and they've come up with a great switch; they want you to play the missionary, and they're hoping Sam Sorel will play the hooker—in drag, naturally—but wearing his own hair."

She sat up slowly, and even that gentle movement almost bounced her global-shaped breasts clean out of the bikini top. "Sam Sorel!" Kewpie-doll blue eyes squinted up at me after she yanked off her cheaters. "What are you? Some kind of nut?"

"Tell you the truth," I said, "Sam sent me. He's worried, wants to know why you're going to kill him one day next week?"

"Kill him?" Her eyes widened, in spite of the bright sunlight. "You've got to be crazy!"

I shook my head reprovingly. "You shouldn't have sent him all those threatening letters. Still and all Sam doesn't hold any grudge. He just wants to be sure he'll live to a ripe old age."

She scrambled up onto her feet, grabbed hold of the beach towel and held it up front of herself like a shield. "You go right on back to Sam and tell him to leave me alone!" Her voice was suddenly caught in a hysterical upsurge. "That's never going to happen again, never! You hear me?"

"I figure they can hear you clear over to the Palisades," I winced. "Take it easy, will you? All I want is—"

"You stay away from me, you creep!"

"Listen," I pleaded and held out my hand toward her.

She took a quick step backward. As her heel came down on the tiled edge of the pool, she slipped. For a moment there, she did a kind of wild folk dance as she tried to regain her balance, then disappeared in a fountain of water. Her head broke the surface long enough for her to scream, "Harv!" with enough decibels in back of it to make her a cinch for the next hog-calling championships—then she disappeared again. I would have dived in and made a heroic rescue, except for the fact she had fallen into the shallow end of the pool; all she had to do to save herself was stand up. Then the ground started to shake and I turned around in time to see the motor court manager heading toward me at a fast run.

"So you were trouble after all, buddy-boy?" He skidded to a stop in front of me, and while I tried to ignore the anticipatory gleam in his eyes, I noticed he wasn't even breathing hard.

"That dame is some kind of a nut," I said bitterly. "I hadn't spoken three words to her before she started screaming her head off."

"Just what kind of words, friend?"

"I told her Sam Sorel sent me to—"

"Sorel?" he snarled. "That explains everything!"

His glittering eyes and expanding triceps explained my immediate future, too. I ducked under his Sunday punch and hit him hard in the solar plexus; it felt like my knuckles had slammed into a stone wall and he didn't even grunt. Then he came charging at me like I had just waved a red cape under his nose. A fast sideways shuffle took me out of his way at the last moment. Unable to stop in time, he let out a frustrated bellow of fury as he hit the water, just as Jackie Slater was surfacing for the fifth or sixth time. They both vanished in a spectacular fountain effect, then Graham floundered onto his feet and started toward the side of the pool, mouthing silent obscenities as he came.

I waited until he had almost hoisted himself out of the water before I put my foot against his chest and pushed him back in. He fell back against the half-drowned starlet, who let out a watery moan of anguish. Then his gentlemanly instincts reacted and he made a frantic grab for her as she started sinking again. She kept right on sinking until she disappeared again, while his hand emerged from under the water clutching a scarlet bikini-top. His hand went under the surface a second time, and this time it reappeared clamped tight onto a sodden mess of silver-blond curls. There was a look of pride on his face as he hauled the livid Jackie Slater onto her feet and displayed the naked magnificence of her jutting breasts to my interested gaze. A moment later he looked vaguely hurt when she hit him straight between the eyes with her small clenched fist.

I looked at the small group of interested motor court occupants who had gathered at the side of the pool and were watching the proceedings with open-mouthed fascination, then looked at Graham.

"Why don't we talk this over, Harv?" I suggested diffidently. "Someplace quiet, where we don't have an audience?"

Five minutes later we were sitting around in Jackie Slater's unit, drinking Scotch. Graham was wearing a dry outfit of knitted shirt and Bermuda shorts, while the starlet was swathed in an enormous tentlike robe, with a towel wrapped turban style around her head. The atmosphere wasn't exactly friendly; from the morose look on his face, I figured Graham could start in slugging again at any time. I carefully explained how one of Sorel's ex-wives was threatening to kill him and I was trying to find out which one before he was just a name in the obituary columns.

"Whoever she is, I hope she gets him," Jackie Slater said tightly. "I'll dance on his grave!"

"You're no cop," Graham said accusingly. "Just who are you, anyway?"

"My name's Holman," I told him. "I'm a kind of troubleshooter."

"So shoot Sam!" the starlet snapped. "He's nothing but trouble."

"Holman?" Graham reflected out loud. "I've heard of you. Some Hollywood big-deal name has a problem, you fix it for them, right?"

"Something like that," I agreed.

"I wish you'd told me earlier." He forced a grin onto his face. "I mean, we wouldn't have had this misunderstanding if I'd known. Honey," he looked at the silver-blonde, "a guy like Mr. Holman wouldn't fool around with a bad joke. This has to be serious."

"So?" She glared at him.

"So let's see what we can do to help Mr. Holman," he said persuasively. "Sorel is a dirty name around here for sure, but nobody is planning to kill him."

"Somebody should!" Jackie Slater ignored his plead-

27

ing glance. "He's not even a man! Did you know that, Mr. Holman? Ten months we were married and he didn't make it at all. Not even on our wedding night!" She laughed scornfully. "Then he had the nerve to get mad at me for taking my fun someplace else. He used to give me the creeps." A sudden shiver disturbed the voluminous robe. "Most nights I couldn't sleep with him crying out the whole time. He used to get these dreadful nightmares, and he was like some little kid, scared out of his skin!"

"What gave him the nightmares?" I asked.

She shrugged. "Who knows? He said he was scared of being shut in anyplace, but I figured it was more like his guilty conscience!"

"Have you seen him since the divorce?"

The hesitation was a second too long before she shook her head. "I wouldn't be seen dead within a mile of Sam."

"Tell him, honey," Graham said.

"There are times, Harv, when I wish you'd mind your own goddamned business," she grated.

"Maybe Mr. Holman knows already," he persisted. "Don't make a liar out of yourself, Jackie. Remember what I said; a guy like him doesn't fool around with a bad joke. If somebody does kill Sorel, you don't want to wind up as the star suspect, do you?"

"I guess not." She didn't sound too sure about that. Her eyes closed for a moment, and I guessed she was seeing the glamorous Jackie Slater, falsely accused of murdering her ex-husband, and tearfully declining the offers of fabulous star contracts until her name had been cleared. "I'm sorry, Mr. Holman." She opened her eyes again and batted her long lashes at me. "I wasn't telling the truth."

"Call me Rick," I suggested.

"Thanks, Rick." Her smile said we were buddies—big deal! "I did see Sam, about a month back. He came visiting one night, unwanted and unexpected! I was so surprised to see him, he was in the living room already before I had a chance to say anything." Her voice went flat. "He's crazy in the head, I guess you know that? He started yelling at me, saying he knew about Harv and me—well, who doesn't?—and he wouldn't stand for an ex-wife of his having an affair with another man. I figured it was all kind of ridiculous and I laughed at him. It was a big mistake, Rick, because the next moment he hit me." Her face became rigid. "He kept on hitting me; he beat the hell out of me. I figure he would have killed me if Harv hadn't come by and tossed him out."

"I tell you, Rick," Graham said in a very sincere voice, "Sorel was like a crazy man. Normally, I would have figured I could have handled him with one hand, but that night it took all I had to get him out of here. I called a doctor for Jackie right away, and he put her under sedation. She was in bed for a whole week."

"The bruises!" Jackie shuddered daintily. "You just should have seen them, Rick." The long lashes batted provocatively at me. "Well, maybe you shouldn't have. I swear, I was black and blue all over. I still have this sinus condition, caused by the beating Sam gave me, and the doctor says it could be permanent."

It was a disaster too horrible to contemplate, so I didn't waste any time trying. "This was around a month back? You remember the exact date?"

"July ninth." Her face became a mask of tragedy. "Will I ever forget it?—my birthday!"

"Is that the only time you've seen Sorel since the divorce?"

She nodded. "Sure, I wouldn't want to see the creep anytime, except in his coffin."

"Jackie?" Graham cleared his throat nervously. "I wish you wouldn't keep on saying things like that." He gave me a glassy smile. "If you keep on, you'll give Rick the wrong impression."

"Don't be a dope, Harv!" She sneered at him. "Sure, I'd like to see Sam dead, but does that mean I'm about to take after him with an ice pick?"

"I guess not," Graham said glumly, then concentrated on his Scotch.

"Any dame who's been married to that creep has my sympathy," Jackie said. "But he's not worth risking your life for, just to get even. Besides, a girl has to think about the alimony check."

"Which is considerable," I ventured.

A complacent look came over her face. "It sure is, and any dame who's been stuck with that creep deserves every penny."

"Do you know either of his other two ex-wives?" I asked.

"No, I never did believe in wakes." Her eyes were cold and calculating as she looked at me for a long moment, then she seemed to make up her mind and turned toward Graham. "Harv," her voice was wheedling, "you love me, don't you?"

"Sure do, honey!"

"You want to marry me right now?"

"Sugar," he sounded like he was trapped, "you know I want that more than anything in the whole goddamned world, but with the lousy money I make managing this morgue, how would we live?"

"It translates like, out goes the alimony check and out goes Harv!" There was a knowing glint in her eyes as she grinned at me. "That answer your question, Rick?"

"I guess it does." I stood up. "Thanks for the drink. Anything develops, I'll let you know."

"I'll walk you to your car." Graham got out of his chair quickly.

"Come back anytime, Rick." There was an open invitation in the starlet's husky voice. "Anytime at all. We can always chitchat about some of the nice influential Hollywood people you know. Not like Sam, I mean."

"I might do that," I said vaguely.

"Harv visits with his mother on Tuesday nights." She sat up in her chair and one fold of the heavy robe fell open, apparently by accident, revealing the heavy swell of her right breast. "So make it a Tuesday night, huh, Rick?"

Graham walked beside me in silence until we reached my car. "She's a bitch, of course," he said heavily. "But she's only the latest in a long line of bitches I've known, which goes right back to my mother."

"What do you want?" I asked him, "sympathy or analysis?"

"I'm not sure I don't want out." He rubbed his finger dubiously along the line of his lower lip. "That night when Sorel beat her up. When I got there, they were still screaming at each other in between his punches. He said something about what the hell did she expect after calling him and throwing the relationship in his face? Jackie said she never called him when I mentioned it later, but who knows when she's telling the truth? Sure, she looks like the usual run of stupid starlets who carry their brains in their bras, but underneath she can be a real bitch! I wouldn't be surprised if she did threaten to kill Sorel, even if it was only for kicks."

"And Tuesday nights you visit with your mother, Harv?" I said gently, then watched his triceps closely but they didn't expand at all.

"You want to try your luck, I don't mind," he grated. "Maybe it's time I got myself off the hook. If she's gotten herself involved in some crazy murder threat, I could get some of the backwash. The owners wouldn't like that!"

"You're all heart, Harv," I told him, then got into the car.

"Rick?" He leaned his head in the open window beside me. "So maybe I don't make myself sound like a nice guy—who is? But I'm being honest, trying to be helpful. If anything does break that involves Jackie, try and keep me out of it, will you?"

"Ask me again," I suggested, "say, a couple of Tuesday nights from now?"

The third ex-wife, Beverly Quillen, wasn't home—home being a plush high-rise building back of the Strip. I took time out for lunch, then tried again. She was still out. When I called the hotel, the operator told me Mr. Sorel always slept until five in the afternoon and it wouldn't be worth her job to disturb him. Miss Mayer had left word she wouldn't be back before eight that evening. So I went home to my little status-symbol house in Beverly Hills, figuring it wasn't my fault nobody would let me do any work. I had an energetic swim—one length of my backyard pool—then lay in the sun for a while. It was nice to play lotus in the land of the lotus once in a while, and my conscience didn't bother me at all. Either my client was a raving psycho case, or I'd just run up against the best bunch of liars in the business. I kept my fingers crossed the potential killer wasn't lying about the time she intended knocking off Sam. If she killed him before the week starting Tuesday, it would destroy my faith in honest murderers.

Around five thirty I had a shower and got dressed again. It figured Beverly Quillen would come home nights, so it was worth giving her another try. An hour later I was starting my second bourbon on the rocks and thinking I should make a move, when the phone rang.

"Mr. Holman?" The voice was recognizable. "This is Linda Galen."

"Miss Galen?" I said politely.

"I have to talk with you." There was an urgency in her deep voice. "Andrea told me about her conversation with you after I left the coffee shop this morning. I think she gave you a one-sided picture. There are other things I should explain to you."

"Go ahead," I told her.

"I can't now, over the phone. Could you come to the apartment later tonight, say around eight thirty?"

"I'll be there."

"Andrea has to be at a small private buyers' showing tonight, and it starts then. She won't be back for at least a couple of hours. And, if I might ask a favor of you, Mr. Holman. I know it sounds stupid but"—her voice faltered for a moment—"would you mind coming in the back way? The service door is never locked before midnight, and I'll leave the back door of the apartment unlocked so you can walk right in. It's just that—well—Andrea's brother lives right across the hall from us and ever since we moved in after that visit from Sam, he's been kind of overly protective. Andrea's sure to tell him she'll be out for a while tonight, so he'll be watching and he could make things awkward if he saw you visiting. He's not the kind of man who'll listen to explanations, and he'd be sure to tell Andrea about your visit, anyway."

"I'll use the back stairs," I said.

"Thank you very much, Mr. Holman. The apartment number is Three *B,* on the third floor, of course." There was a couple of seconds' silence before she spoke again, in a warm voice. "I've been quite stupid, Mr. Holman. I should have realized before that you're the only one I can possibly trust now." Then she hung up.

I filled in the next couple of hours the easiest way I know how, with an early dinner on Restaurant Row. Eating at that time, the waiter obviously figured, made me either an escaped con or the loneliest guy in the whole world. Then I drove out to West Hollywood and parked the car a block from where Linda Galen lived. The apartment building was on a nondescript street, and I found my way around to the service area in back. After navigating around four slightly high trash cans, I found, like she had told me, that the service door wasn't locked. I climbed the dimly lit back stairs to the third floor and saw 3B was right across the landing. The door was slightly open, so I pushed it farther open, then stepped inside the apartment.

The faint light filtering through the doorway showed I was in the pint-sized kitchen. I called out, "Miss Galen?" and waited. She didn't answer, so I tried a couple more times, with the same result. There were three possible explanations, I figured; she was out, asleep—or dead. It would be best to make sure, I told myself dismally, and pretended I hadn't noticed the small hairs twitching at the nape of my neck. I walked into the darkness to the other side of the kitchen, and ran my hand down the wall until I found the light-switch. The living room was tastefully furnished in a very feminine style, and empty. So were the bathroom and the first of the two bedrooms, I discovered within the next ten seconds. Then I found Linda Galen in the second bedroom.

She was lying diagonally across the bed, sprawled out on her back, still wearing that silk dress with the alternate brown and orange stripes, only now it didn't

33

look elegant anymore. It was bunched up tight around her waist, brutally exposing her naked body in all its vulnerability. The top of the dress had been ripped apart and blood still oozed slowly from the many stab wounds in her breasts. On either side of her rib cage, the bedcover was stained with large patches of glistening wetness. Her features were twisted into a look of unendurable terror, while her dark-brown eyes stared fixedly at the ceiling in mute appeal. Her underclothing was scattered across the floor, and a blood-stained carving-knife lay on the cushion beside her head. Only the lacquered, shiny black helmet of her hair remained completely undisturbed, and it somehow added an extra macabre element to the scene of violent death.

I automatically checked my watch and saw it was twenty of nine. She couldn't have been dead very long. Logic said she must have been murdered between the time Andrea Marco left for her fashion showing and the time I arrived. Unless—there was also an obvious alternative—Andrea herself had killed Linda Galen. I retraced my steps, used a pocket handkerchief on the lightswitch in the living room, and carefully wiped the back doorknob clean on my way out. There was nobody around when I walked through the service area, and I didn't meet anybody in the street on my way back to the car. Nobody who had been involved with Linda Galen would remain anonymous for long, but I needed all the time I could get, so I decided to let somebody else find the body and call the police.

CHAPTER FOUR

The front door of the apartment opened, and a pair of deep blue eyes looked at me with casual interest. They belonged to a tall redhead. Her titian hair was cut real short, then brushed forward from the crown of her head, leaving her delicately shaped ears exposed while concealing her high forehead with bangs. The style suited her prominent cheekbones and firmly rounded jaw. Her nose was a little too short, her mouth a little too wide, but all-in-all it was both a highly intelligent and highly attractive face. She was wearing a white shirt and a pair of the shortest shorts I had ever seen. The long tanned legs were lithe and graceful, and her small breasts thrust against the cotton fabric of her shirt with pointed impudence.

"I was in the middle of my setting-up exercises," she said easily. "Not expecting anyone to visit tonight. This is my night for concentrating on the body-skinny, and the hell with my mind!"

"I'm Rick Holman," I said, "and I—"

"—want to know why I'm planning on killing Sam Sorel sometime next week," she finished for me. "You'd better come on in."

I followed her through the entrance hall into the living room, which looked vaguely Oriental and maybe would have reminded some myopic Japanese of home. She gestured for me to sit down on the couch, then sat down beside me and sprawled her long legs out comfortably in front of her.

"I got a rambling and incoherent call from Sam

around six thirty tonight," she said. "He was loaded, of course. I figured that story about one of his ex-wives threatening to kill him was pure fantasy, and Rick Holman strictly a figment of his alcoholic imagination. So it looks like I'm wrong on both counts." She smiled suddenly, showing a couple of cute, but crooked, front teeth. "I am Beverly Quillen, incidentally, if you were wondering."

"It's just that I'm trying to get my breath back," I told her.

"You should do some setting-up exercises along with me. You're much too young for shortness of breath." Her fist suddenly rapped my chest. "It doesn't sound hollow or anything. Could it be my dazzling beauty that makes you suddenly breathless?"

"I guess it's more the way you run off at the mouth the whole time," I said truthfully.

"Blunt, to the point of rudeness!" She clasped her hands behind her head and leaned back. "I like that in a man. Shows decisiveness, and that's getting to be a rare quality these days in our organization-mad society."

"Wasn't that one of Sam's big problems during your marriage?" I growled. "You drove him crazy, analyzing him the whole time, and when you finally started taking his special brand of humor apart, it was more than he could stand?"

"What Sam needed all along was not only an analyst, but also a mother, a lover, and a servant—all rolled into one person," she said evenly. "For me, the analyst was a cinch. I think, for a while there, I even made the grade as a lover; but I was the world's biggest drop-out with the mother and servant bits. Don't you think he was just a little too demanding, Mr. Holman?"

"Don't you think you were just a little too bad-tempered?" I countered. "Trying to stab him with a carving-knife, and all?"

Her face stiffened a little. "Sam told you that?"

"Who else? He even showed me the scar on his wrist to prove it."

"Just the one wrist?" Her voice was faintly mocking. "He staged the big farewell scene; good-bye cruel

36

world, and even more-cruel wife! But he set it up at a time when he was sure I'd walk into the bathroom within five minutes, and he didn't slash his wrists very deeply. Not deep enough to cut a vein or an artery, or anything really unpleasant like that. Just so he broke the skin, and even a little blood mixed with the water in the bath can look most impressive."

"You're saying it was a suicide attempt?"

"Sam wanted it to look that way. I imagine he hoped it might bring out the mother and servant in me. It had gotten so he was sulking about his nightmares because I always tried to figure out the deeper reasons for them instead of holding him in my arms and crooning nursery rhymes in his pink ear. The vast majority of claustrophobes never have nightmares once they're grown up, did you know that? Not unless they suffer some severe claustrophobic experience in their adult life which creates fresh trauma."

"You're trying to say whatever caused his nightmares, it wasn't his claustrophobia?" I cleverly suggested.

She nodded. "The original cause of his phobia goes back to his childhood, when his lovely mother once locked him inside a trunk for an hour as punishment for something. Sam identifies with this. But normal adults who suffer from some special phobia—and who doesn't—are careful to avoid getting into situations where they risk being subjected to their special phobias. The claustrophobe doesn't explore caves, for example, or become a miner. Sam is just the originial neurosis kid. You name it, he's got it."

"You majored in psychology, I take it?"

"I did, indeed. Right now I'm assisting on an experimental psychology project at U.C.L.A. and it's fascinating."

"Have you seen Sam since your divorce?"

"A couple of weeks back. Around nine one evening I opened the door and there he was. Very drunk, and in a very bad temper. He talked up a storm about how he knew I had been through a succession of affairs with different men since the divorce. I said that was perfectly true, and so what? Living is just an experiment after all, and I wasn't about to get caught up in a wrong marriage for a second time. Then he went berserk. Raved on about no ex-wife of his was going to live like a whore, and by the time he'd finished with me I wouldn't be able to attract anyone except a plastic surgeon. The next thing I knew, he was using physical violence."

"He beat you up?"

She chuckled softly. "Not exactly! I have a fetish about physical fitness, and Sam has never been a physically active person. He was also very drunk at the time. I just dodged out of his way, then hit him over the head with a heavy ashtray, and he passed out cold. I called a cab and bribed the driver to take my drunken friend home. It wasn't even messy, although it did shatter the ashtray and I was a little annoyed about that. Venetian glass is so expensive."

"You haven't seen him since?"

"No, and I don't imagine I will after what happened that night. Sam is a very devout coward."

"This is some apartment," I said, looking around. "I guess the rent comes high?"

"It takes most of the alimony check, but with the money I earn I have enough to get by. Can we use first names, or are you always formal when you talk with potential murderesses?"

"I'm never formal with redheads, Beverly," I assured her.

"I'm glad to hear it, Rick. Do you mind if I finish my exercises while we talk?"

"Be my guest."

She stretched out on the rug, her feet facing me, then jackknifed her legs high in the air and began pedaling. It made concentration hard, watching the taut rounded cheeks of her bottom oscillating in a fast rhythm just a few feet away from where I was sitting.

"Do you know either of Sorel's other ex-wives?" I asked finally.

"No." She stopped pedaling and lay flat on the floor for a moment, then came up into a sitting position, leaned forward, and touched her toes without any apparent effort. "I wouldn't want to, either. Not after the way Sam used to drive me up the wall talking about his first wife. From what he said about Linda, she was all those women he wanted, and more, all rolled into one. I could never figure out why he divorced her if she was that good, and one day I made the mistake of saying just that to him. He didn't speak to me for a month. It was my fault; I should have remembered Sam never made a mistake. It's other people's mistakes that get wished onto him, if you get what I mean. Everything that's ever happened to him has always been somebody else's fault."

"I wonder you married him in the first place, Beverly?"

"Me, too." Her voice was muffled as she now lay on her stomach, raising one arm and leg into the air alternately. "I think I was in the father-complex stage at the time. Besides, he was rich and famous, and that made him kind of exciting. I was madly in love with the idea of being in love with him, and—you know—fancy the famous Sam Sorel wanting to marry little ole me!" She rolled over onto her back again and sat up. "You're some kind of private detective, Rick?"

"Some kind," I agreed.

"Is it exciting? I mean, maybe it's dangerous sometimes, and you must meet all kinds of fascinating people." She took a deep breath and lifted her arms above her head, then exhaled slowly. "What do you think about me? Am I fascinating and exciting?"

"I think you're a kook," I said truthfully, "and if you figured you had good reason for killing Sorel, you'd go right ahead and try."

"Really?" She rolled over again and did ten push-ups the hard way, with her stomach never actually touching the rug. "But I don't have a good reason, do I?"

"If you did, it could be a challenge to tell me, then go right ahead; see if you could murder Sam, and still get away with it."

She flopped back onto the couch beside me, then smiled slowly. "I'm the one who's supposed to know about experimental psychology, Rick! But, for a shot in the dark, it's shrewd character analysis. Suppose I told you the only man I've ever really loved was about to marry me until Sam got to him and told him a whole bunch of lies? But Sam was so convincing this man believed him and took off into the wild blue yonder. Would you believe that was a motive good enough for me to want to kill Sam?"

"Maybe." I shrugged. "But I'd want to check the details."

"Suppose Sam told him I was a nympho, and proved it because it's true. That would make my motivation even stronger, wouldn't it?"

"With you, I guess it would."

"His name is Roger Hugill, and he lives in Brentwood, or did until he ran out of my life last week. Sam had to get even for me bouncing that ashtray off his head, and he sure did. Check it out, why don't you?"

"What's the Brentwood address?"

"I'm not about to make it too easy for you, Rick. Find out. Ask Sam about it, why don't you?" She turned toward me suddenly and put her hand on my thigh. "I find you very attractive, Rick. Do you find me the same?"

"Sure," I nodded.

"You don't sound wildly enthusiastic!" She got up from the couch in an impatient manner, walked maybe four steps, then turned back toward me. "You think I'm kidding about the nympho thing, don't you?"

"I wish," I said fervently, "just once, you'd say something without making it into a goddamned question the whole time!"

"Now you're irritated." She grinned nastily. "That means you're nervous, and you're trying to hide it. I wonder if the thought of me being a nympho excites you, or just scares the hell out of you?" The blue of her eyes seemed to deepen as she gave me a somber stare. "Why don't we find out?"

I watched blankly as she unbuttoned her white shirt and pulled it off, then unzipped the shorts and let them fall around her ankles. She started back toward the couch, wearing only a white bra—the cups punctuated by the hard-tipped thrust of her small breasts—and white mini briefs straddling her lean hips. There was a warm gleam in her eyes and a soft purring sound came from someplace deep in her throat. I had a strong instinctive feeling that it was important to outsmart her right then. There was no logic in back of the thought, just an urgent insistence from my subconscious.

I got up from the couch and took a quick step toward her. She seemed to waver for a moment, but it was too late to change her mind. My hands were already on her hips. A split second later they were cupped around the cheeks of her bottom, the fingers sinking deep into the firm flesh and forcing her body hard up against mine. Then I sank my teeth urgently into her lower lip and held it clamped tight. Her reaction was instantaneous and violent. The room rocked dizzily as her clenched fists slammed against the sides of my head, just in back of my ears. I let go of everything my hands and teeth had been holding onto so tight.

She backed away from me fast, a shocked expression on her face, until she reached the spot where she had dropped her clothes. The way she scrambled back into her shorts, you would have figured they were some kind of chain-metal chastity belt guaranteed to keep the wolves away from—well—keep them at bay.

"You know something, Beverly?" I rubbed the aching sides of my head tenderly. "I believe you're a nympho, the way I believe in a guy called Roger Hugill!"

"You're nothing but an animal!" She thrust her arms into the shirt and started buttoning it down the front with uncertain fingers.

"That's real sophisticated talk from a psychology major!" I sneered. "The next time you get cute and try and second-guess me, you'd better be right, huh?"

"Will you please get the hell out of here?" she wailed in a despairing voice.

"You're fresh out of heavy ashtrays?"

The look on her face suggested she might try for a carving-knife from the kitchen, so I waved her a tentative farewell and left.

It was just after ten when I arrived at the exclusive club where Sam Sorel would soon be making his final

41

performance of his three weeks' season. By the look of the crowd milling around, he would be playing to a full room, and then some. I went around to the dressing room, knocked, and this time waited for somebody to ask me in.

"Who in hell is that?" Sorel's voice snarled from inside.

"Holman," I said.

"Oh!" He obviously tried to make his voice sound more pleasant. "Come right on in, Rick."

Sorel was sitting in his favorite chair in front of the dresser mirror, wearing a faded robe. The glass was in his hand, the bottle by his right elbow, and his deep-set dark-brown eyes looked like they were silently weeping for the whole world.

Sonia Mayer was wearing a knockout of a dress that came in two tiers; the first was plain black, and form-fitting all the way from where it started low on her breasts to where it finished high on her thighs. The second tier was an overlay of sheer lace, twinkling with sequins, that added a luster to the bare swell of her breasts beneath, and to the roundness of her knees and deepening thighs. The tiny copper bell still dangled from one naked earlobe and it tinkled as she turned her head toward me.

"Hi, Rick." Her smooth contralto sounded impersonal. "What's new?"

"All that's new to me is old hat to Sam." I pushed the door shut and leaned against it. "If he'd told me some things last night it would have saved me a hell of a lot of walking around today."

He savored a mouthful of bourbon for a while before he finally swallowed it. "I don't dig you, Rick."

"Sam Sorel, the raging tornado," I said bleakly. "Sam Sorel, the moral crusader. Sam Sorel, the rapist—the guy who beats up his ex-wives—need I go on?"

"Rick"—Sonia's voice was icy-cold—"have you flipped?"

"It's possible." I nodded toward Sorel's back. "Ask him."

I watched his reflection and saw his skin pucker into a million more wrinkles as he grimaced sharply. Then he ran one hand slowly through his long graying hair. "It's been a long, hard day, friend. All those people out there waiting for my big final performance in the club. I mean, a guy should give of his best, right? So can't it wait?"

"Why not?" I shrugged. "Who in hell cares if you get murdered next week?"

"Sam, honey." Sonia's voice sounded so maternal I wouldn't have been surprised to see a line of small triplets suddenly bounce onto her knee. "I'll take Rick outside and talk it over with him. We'll see you back here after the show—okay?"

"Okay." He poured himself another drink and his hand was shaking enough for the bottle to play a tuneless refrain against the side of the glass. "You just remember, whatever he tells you, Sonia, it's only his side of it."

"Sure, Sam." She got up from her chair and walked over to him, then rubbed the back of his neck affectionately. "When did I ever stop listening to you?"

He took her hand in his and kissed the back of it gently. "You're the only one who's ever understood," he said thickly.

"Don't worry." She withdrew her hand easily. "You just go out there and knock 'em dead!"

Sorel stared back at his own reflection again. "If I'm so goddamned funny why don't I ever make myself laugh?"

Sonia Mayer opened the door and waited for me to go first. We walked down to the end of the corridor in silence, then she stopped. "We can't talk in the club. Do you know any other place near here?"

"There's a bar just a block down," I told her. "They have a man who plays quiet piano. People go there for drinking, mostly."

"That sounds fine."

She tucked her arm through mine and I was immediately conscious of the soft contour of her left breast pressing against my elbow. I would have liked to go the long way around—like through Santa Monica first— but the block ran out in no time at all, and she withdrew her arm as we entered the bar. The waiter put us in a secluded alcove; I ordered bourbon for me and a stinger for her. We listened to the piano improvising its way through a bunch of old standards until the drinks were served.

I looked at the two glasses sitting in front of us, hers taller than mine, and watched a bit of ice melt down into the bourbon. I wondered quietly to myself which traumatic experience made Sam Sorel drink so much.

"Sam Sorel: moral crusader, rapist, the guy who beats up his ex-wives?" Her gray-green eyes widened as she looked hard at me. "You're the one with the fancy words, Rick!"

"Tell me something. Where was Sam the second Friday in May, on July ninth, and a couple of weeks back?"

"Is this some kind of gag?"

I shook my head.

"Well, the last one's easy. He was right here in L.A. a couple of weeks back. I need a little time to remember the other two."

"I'll wait," I said.

"It's that important?" The little copper bell called to me as she tilted her head and concentrated on the low ceiling for a few seconds. "July ninth, I'm almost certain we were here then. Just for a couple of days to get the details set on the picture deal. It was Chicago in May; Sam was playing the Emperor Room there. No, hold everything! He didn't open there until the fourteenth, a Tuesday. The weekend before, I don't know where he was because he suddenly decided to take off by himself on Thursday to commune with his comic muse, or something."

"So he could have come back to L.A.?"

"I guess so. Why is it so important, Rick?"

I told her about his visits to the three ex-wives, and what they claimed had happened while Sorel was with them. She listened attentively until I was all through, without the slightest change in facial expression.

"I just don't know." She sipped her drink for a moment. "Maybe it did happen like they said. I can't see why Sam would be bothered. His ex-wives were dead and buried as far as he was concerned, until those

44

letters started arriving. I know it's a wild idea, but could the three of them have gotten together in some kind of conspiracy against Sam?"

"It's wild, and maybe possible," I admitted. "That list you gave me. Who gave you their addresses?"

"Sam, of course. I guess he got them from his attorneys."

"Andrea Marco said they moved out of Linda Galen's apartment, into her place, the day after Sam's visit. They figured they'd both be safer there. So it also figures they wouldn't have given Sam's attorneys the new address. But Sam gave it to you?"

"You make it sound bad, Rick, but there could be a dozen logical explanations, and are you sure they didn't give it to Sam's attorneys?"

I grinned wryly. "You're just biased because you're in love with him, Sonia!"

"Not in the way you mean," she said coolly.

"You sure could have fooled me last night when I walked back into the dressing room to pick up that list," I sneered.

"Sam is a very great talent." Her contralto voice was still completely self-possessed. "A very great talent sometimes needs very special handling. I give him that, Rick."

"Maybe it's none of my business," I said grudgingly, "but I'd like to make you some of my business."

"I'd prefer you concentrate on seeing that Sam stays alive through next week." She smiled briefly. "Then, maybe, we could talk about it afterward?"

"Okay," I said in a reluctant voice. "You're without a doubt the most beautiful carrot I've ever had dangled under my nose. I guess that's something?"

"I don't think it's worth your while to try and talk to him after his performance tonight," she said. "There'll be a whole mob of people in the dressing room, and an all-night party afterward most likely. Why don't you come around late in the morning and work it out?"

"Why not?" I couldn't tell her that any time now Sam would be busy working things out with the cops. "You're moving out to the house in Brentwood then?"

Sonia nodded. "That's why I said make it late, so we can get established. You have the address, it's on the list I gave you."

"The house belongs to a friend, you said. I never did ask his name."

"Roger Hugill," she said casually. "He's an old friend of mine. I'm not sure if Sam has ever met him."

"Is that right?" I stared at her blankly for a moment. "What does he do?"

"He's rich. I know he's a silent partner in a couple of outfits—Reynor Projects, the plastics people—and the Trushman Detective Agency—maybe a dozen more for all I know. Does it matter?"

"I'm always curious about people who lend their houses to somebody who's threatened with murder. Is he out of town?"

"No. He's a bachelor and lives alone, except for a housekeeper. The house is big enough for the three of us to live in for a couple of weeks without getting in each other's hair."

"I've had some dealings with the Trushman Agency, but I never heard his name mentioned."

She shrugged impatiently. "Like I told you, he's a silent partner. Puts up half the capital and takes half the profit. Sometimes I wish I had a deal like that."

"Don't we all?" I agreed.

"Are you going to walk me back to the club, Rick?" She finished her drink then looked at me expectantly. "I have to get back before Sam is on; it's a kind of ritual between us on opening and closing nights."

"Sure." I waved for the check. "I guess being Sam Sorel's personal manager is a full-time job?"

"It's not so much a job as a lifetime of dedication!" The sudden smile lit up her whole face. "Still and all, I wouldn't trade it for anything else in the whole world."

She didn't take my arm on the walk back to the club, and I would have resented it if I hadn't had a whole bunch of other problems on my mind.

CHAPTER FIVE

The front door of the house in Brentwood opened a couple of seconds after I had rung the doorbell, and a tall guy in his early forties stood there glowering at me. His thick brown hair was brushed stiffly back from his forehead; the cold gray eyes and the bristling moustache gave him a vaguely military look. He was wearing the kind of suit that's a steal at three hundred bucks. Somehow, I got the impression he was just back from a summit meeting and his vote had decided them to close down Fort Knox immediately.

"Mr. Hugill?" I said.

"Yes?" His voice was harsh and impatient.

"I'm Rick Holman and I'd like to talk with you."

"What about?"

"A mutual friend, Sonia Mayer." I decided Hugill was the kind of guy you can dislike at first meeting and I already did. "We have a mutual problem, like keeping Sam Sorel alive while he's your house guest."

"All right," he said grudgingly. "I suppose we had better talk inside."

I followed him into a large living room which was cluttered with early Colonial furniture. The walls were plastered with oil paintings of every conceivable bird species, and some that hadn't been nightmared yet. Hugill placed himself in front of me with hands clasped behind his back and glared like I was a class of one awaiting instruction.

"I know of your reputation, Holman," he barked. "I

therefore presume this is not some kind of a bad joke."

"One of Sorel's three ex-wives is threatening to kill him any day from Tuesday on," I said. "He takes it seriously and I'm inclined to go along with him. I figured, since you're involved, we should have a talk."

His moustache bristled for a moment. "You're concerned about protecting Sorel while he's a guest in my home, of course?"

"I'm more concerned that one of his ex's is Beverly Quillen, the girl you were about to marry until—so she says—Sam Sorel got to you with a whole bunch of lies about her."

"What?" His eyes popped. "That's sheer nonsense!"

"So you say," I said in a reasonable voice. "Beverly Quillen says different. So, will the real, congenital liar please stand up?"

His face darkened and I wondered if he was about to call out the guard and have me thrown in the tank for insubordination. Then he blinked slowly, cleared his throat a couple of times, and almost managed a smile.

"There must be something going on here I don't understand. I don't know anyone by the name of Beverly Quillen, and I never have. My only connection with Sorel is through Sonia Mayer."

"How did you get to know her?"

"I met her before she became Sorel's personal manager. I happened to have a small interest in the talent agency where she was working then, and I met her there. We kept up our friendship after she took over Sorel, so when she called and explained how he needed someplace quiet to rest up between finishing his club engagement and starting work on a motion picture, I was happy to agree to the both of them staying in my house during the intervening period."

Underneath all that stuffed-shirt pomposity, I sourly figured, who the hell could tell if he was lying? "You know Linda Galen or Jackie Slater?" I asked him. "Sorel's other two ex-wives?"

48

"Definitely not!" he snapped. "I've already made it clear to you, Holman, that my only connection with Sorel is through my friendship with Sonia."

"Just how friendly were you, during her talent agency days?" I leered at him, in case my tone of voice didn't make the innuendo obvious.

"Our friendship was purely platonic." His face darkened again. "Goddammit, Holman! This is outrageous! I'm not about to tolerate you questioning me as if I'm some kind of criminal. You can—"

The phone rang, cutting him off in mid-thunder. He gave a frustrated snort, then walked across the room to where the phone stood on a hideous table.

"Hugill!" he shouted into the receiver. Then his face softened. "Why, hello, Sonia. . . . Who?" His bushy eyebrows lifted a quarter inch. "Yes, he is here. Hold the line." He stared at me suspiciously. "It's Sonia, she wants to talk with you, Holman." He handed me the phone reluctantly, like it was the key to some top-secret code.

"Rick?" Sonia's voice sounded tearful. "Something dreadful has happened. Linda Galen was murdered tonight!"

"What?" I tried hard to sound real surprised.

"The police are here at the club now, waiting to interview Sam as soon as he finishes his performance. I've tried to explain about the murder threats and everything, but they want to see the actual letters."

"You told the police I've got them?"

"Yes, Rick. They want you to come over to the club right away."

"I'll do that," I said with no enthusiasm at all. "Who's in charge of the investigation?"

"A Lieutenant Santana." Her voice had a hopeful note to it. "Do you know the lieutenant?"

"We've met." A painful spasm clutched at my intestines as I remembered the last time I'd met Santana; we had wound up in a slugging match. "Tell him I'll be there in fifteen minutes."

"Thanks, Rick."

I hung up. Hugill was watching me expectantly, like a bird dog, and I waited for him to bark loudly, then point. After a few seconds I shook my head and said in a somber voice, "It's bad! One of Sorel's ex-wives has been murdered tonight."

"That's terrible!" He sounded genuinely shocked.

"Poor Beverly Quillen," I muttered.

"Beverly?" His voice cracked.

I studied his gray face and pained eyes for a long moment, then shrugged as I lied. "She must have been completely wrong about Linda Galen."

"What in hell are you babbling about now?" He almost screamed the words at me.

"Now that Linda Galen has been murdered," I said patiently, "she can't be the prime suspect for Sorel's potential murderess, the way Beverly figured."

For a moment there he looked like he was about to choke to death in front of my eyes. Then he ground out the words, slowly and painfully. "You're telling me Linda Galen was murdered tonight—not Beverly?"

"Of course." I lifted my eyebrows a fraction. "Whatever gave you that idea?"

"You and your goddamned doubletalk!" he snarled.

"Why should you worry who was murdered?" I smiled at him warmly. "You don't even know anybody called Beverly Quillen."

"Just get the hell out of my house, Holman." His moustache bristled violently. "Before I throw you out bodily!"

"I am the kind of man who can take a hint," I said with great dignity, "and I think all your lousy pictures are strictly for the birds."

It wasn't exactly a good exit line, but thinking about Lieutenant Santana had made me nervous. I thought about him during the drive back to the club and all I got was even more nervous. A uniformed cop in the foyer told me the lieutenant was in the manager's office, and how to get there.

Santana didn't look any different from the last time I had seen him, and that wasn't reassuring at all. He was still a guy around fifty years old, average height and weight, and an average amount of thinning black hair on his scalp, slowly graying back from the temples. His face still looked like it had been hewn from stone with a blunt pickax, and his brown eyes still glittered with a basic contempt for the whole goddamned world, and maybe a little extra for me personally. He was sitting in back of the manager's desk, with its cluttered accumulation of unanswered letters and unpaid bills, like he belonged there.

There were three other people inside the office. Andrea Marco was sitting on the couch, red-eyed, staring stonily into space. Beside her, a big flabby-looking guy somewhere in his mid-twenties was nervously smoking a cigarette and occasionally shaking the long blond hair out of his eyes. Sonia Mayer gave me a tentative smile of welcome from a stiff-backed chair on the opposite side of the room.

"Well," Santana said softly, "I guess we can all relax now that Holman is here."

I walked over to the desk, took the threatening letters out of my wallet, and dropped them on the desk in front of him. "How have you been, Lieutenant?"

"Happy," he grunted, "until I heard your name mentioned." He took his time about reading each letter in turn, then pushed them to one side. "You know Miss Marco, I understand?" I nodded. "Her brother, Frank?"

"Hi, Mr. Holman," the flabby guy said in a high-pitched voice. He started to smile at me, took a quick sideways glance at his sister's rigid face, then changed his mind.

Santana yawned openly, then looked at Sonia. "How much longer do we get to wait for the funny man to finish?"

"It should be soon now," she told him in her warm contralto voice. "But this is his closing night here, Lieutenant. They won't want to let him go."

"I saw him on television one time," he said bleakly. "He didn't make me laugh."

"Has anything—ever?" I wondered out loud.

"Only you, Holman." He looked across at the couch. "What time did you say it was when you got back to the apartment and found Miss Galen's body?"

51

"Ten thirty," Andrea said in a dull, lifeless voice. "I've told you that five times already."

He nodded agreement. "The coroner figures it happened sometime between eight and nine P.M. Where were you then?"

"At the fashion preview, and that's for the fifth time, too!"

"Yeah," he nodded again. "How about you, Holman? Where were you between eight and nine tonight?"

"At home," I lied. "I went out a little after nine to visit with one of Sorel's ex-wives—Beverly Quillen—then I came here and had a drink with Miss Mayer."

"You were home alone?" His mouth twisted a little. "I mean, like all by yourself?"

"All by myself," I agreed.

"It figures you wouldn't have any alibi. I should know something smells about any case you're involved in; even something apart from you, I mean."

"It's the power complex," I said to Sonia. "Give some guys an itty-bitty badge and the next thing you know, they go berserk!"

There was a knock on the door. A uniformed cop pushed it open, stood to one side to let Sorel into the room, then closed the door again. Sonia got up quickly from her chair and ran across to him.

"Sam, honey." Her voice was a caress. "Don't take it too hard, huh?"

"I'm okay," he muttered.

She took his arm and led him to the nearest armchair. He slumped down into it, yanked his string tie loose, then unbuttoned the collar of his jazzy evening shirt. His eyes had a muddy look and seemed to have sunken even deeper into their sockets. There was also a gray pallor under his wrinkled skin. Suddenly Sam Sorel looked fifteen years older than his rightful age.

"I need a drink," he muttered.

"Later!" Santana snapped.

Sorel looked at him irritably. "Who the hell are you?"

"This is Lieutenant Santana," I volunteered. "He never did think you were funny, Sam."

"Neither did I." Sorel shrugged gently. "But what use is the two of us against the rest of the world?"

The lieutenant shot me a cold glance which said for me to keep my big mouth shut, then looked at Sam again. "Where were you around eight tonight?" he barked.

"At Linda's apartment," the comic told him. "She called me about a half hour earlier, said she wanted to see me and"—he pointed his index finger at Andrea Marco—"that the bitch would be out, so we could talk."

"You saw her?"

Sorel shook his head, very carefully, like he was scared it could fall off his shoulders any time now. "No, I didn't see her. That fag"—his index finger pointed at Andrea's brother—"met me in the hallway and said I wasn't getting in. We argued for a couple of minutes but he's some kind of a nut like his sister! He pulled a knife on me and I got scared he'd use it, so I left."

"Lieutenant!" Frank Marco looked at Santana with a boyish smile dimpling his pudgy cheeks. "That's absolutely fantastic! I mean, I never had any knife. I just warned him he wasn't getting inside the apartment, that's all. Especially after the last time he visited with Linda and my sister and nearly killed the both of them! Well, I just wasn't about to—"

"Sure." Santana cut him off in mid-sentence and the boyish smile crumpled a little. "You left?" He looked at the comic for a long moment. "Where did you go then?"

"Back to the hotel."

"You're lying! You went around to the back of the apartment building and came in through the service door—it wasn't locked—then you went up the back stairs and into the apartment through the rear door. It was open when Miss Marco got home. Then you stabbed Linda Galen to death."

"No!" Sam closed his eyes tight shut. "No, I went straight back to the hotel. I couldn't have killed Linda. I loved her, don't you understand? I wanted for us to get married again."

"That isn't even funny!" Andrea said in a remote voice. "The first time he saw her, in all the years since they had been divorced, was three months back. I was there when he stormed into her apartment like a maniac, knocked me unconscious and"—her foice faltered momentarily—"brutally raped Linda. Tonight was only the second time he'd seen her since the divorce, and he murdered her. If that's love, he must be even more crazy than I figured!"

"Tell them, Sonia," Sam whispered, his eyes still tight shut.

"It's true," his personal manager corroborated. "Ever since that first time three months back when Sam lost his temper and became violent, he's realized that he had been in love with Linda all the time. I know they've gotten together whenever they had the chance, but it was very difficult for them. Andrea Marco is a very possessive person, so they could only meet when she wasn't around, and that wasn't often. It had gotten to the point where Linda was so scared of what Andrea Marco and her brother might do if they found out about her relationship with Sam that she was too scared to let Sam help her."

"You dirty, lying bitch!" Andrea said, emphasizing each word. "Linda never loved anyone but me and—"

"Shut up!" Santana told her, without raising his voice. "Miss Mayer, did you ever see Linda Galen with Sorel at any time during the last three months?"

Sonia hesitated, then shook her head. "No, Lieutenant."

"Did you ever talk with her on the phone?"

"No, never."

"So how do you know it's true?"

"Sam told me all about it." Her gray-green eyes were troubled as she looked away from him.

"Of course it will be so lonely for her without Sam!" Andrea said acidly. "No job, nobody to warm her bed, and no more being a big-deal personal manager for a top comic!"

Santana stared at her coldly. "You," he rasped, "and your brother can go. Tell the officer outside where I can find both of you tomorrow; there'll be more questions."

"I'm not going." A look of fixed determination showed on her face. "Not until I've seen you arrest Sorel for Linda's murder."

"Out!" Santana barked.

Frank Marco stood up quickly, then took his sister's arm and pulled her onto her feet. "Come on, Sis," he pleaded. "You can't argue with the lieutenant."

"I have to know!" She pulled her arm free and glared at him. "Don't you understand that, Frank? I have to know he will be punished for killing Linda."

"Get her out of here now," Santana grated, "or I'll have an officer carry her outside."

Marco reached hesitantly for his sister's arm, and she backhanded him viciously across the mouth. While he whimpered in pained shock, she walked stiffly across the room to the door. Marco caught up with her as she stepped out into the corridor, his whole body trembling and blood trickling down his chin from where her ring had cut his lower lip. The lieutenant waited a while after the door had closed in back of them, then looked at Sonia.

"I guess I won't need you anymore, either, Miss Mayer."

"How about Sam?" she asked.

"Him, I need!"

"Very well." She went over to the armchair and rested her hand on Sorel's shoulder for a moment. "I'll wait for you in the dressing room, Sam."

Her eyes, a look of desperate appeal in them, found mine for a moment; then she went out of the office. Santana lit a cigarette and gestured for me to sit down in the chair she had just vacated.

"All right, kiddies," he growled. "So now you both unburden your little hearts, even if we have to stay right here for the rest of the night." He glared at Sorel. "You hired Holman, so I want you to hear everything he tells me. You're his client, so the same goes for him, too." He stabbed his cigarette at me. "You start."

I told him about seeing the three ex-wives, and the gist of their conversations. What I didn't tell him, of course, was how Linda Galen had called and said to meet her in the apartment, and how she was dead when I got there. I didn't tell him about the probable relationship between Beverly Quillen and Hugill, either, because a cop is entitled to do some work on his own account. He mashed the stub of his cigarette in the desk ashtray when I had finished and looked at Sorel.

"You want to plead insanity or something?"

"What?" Sam blinked a couple of times, made an effort, then brought the lieutenant into focus.

"Three months back you go see your first ex-wife, and I've got the Marco dame's description of what happened then. About six weeks back you go visit with your second ex-wife and beat the hell out of her. Two weeks ago"—the lieutenant tried hard to make it sound like a nonchalant phrase—"you would have beat up your third ex-wife, but you were loaded and she didn't panic. You want to deny any of this, Sorel?"

"You don't understand, Lieutenant," Sam said in a thick voice. "You just don't know what it's like!"

"You're so right, I don't understand," Santana rapped. "You want to tell me about it?"

"When I married Jackie Slater I was on the skids and going down fast," Sam said. "At the time we were divorced I was at the end of the line, with no place else to go. But I kept up the alimony payments to all three of them the whole time. For a while there I even hocked my future to keep up those payments, and what kind of gratitude did I ever get from the three of them? Sonia helped me fight my way back to the top again, and I tried not to even think of my three ex's! Then Linda called me long distance in Chicago; she made it real clear just what kind of relationship she had with that Marco bitch and that it was vastly superior to the relationship she'd had with me during the time we were married. So I flipped. Who wouldn't? I remembered how I'd sweated to keep up those alimony payments, and for what? Somehow, I figured, I had to get even!"

"And we know just how you evened the score," Santana said. "How about the other two?"

"Jackie Slater called and gave me a rundown on her

nympho life." Sam's voice thickened with emotion. "On exactly how the various guys she shacked up with treated her. Anything, she said, was better than being married to a no good old man like me—and would I make sure the alimony kept coming in on time."

"So you went and beat her up." The lieutenant sounded bored. "How about Beverly Quillen?"

"That was a goddamned lie about me visiting with her!" Sorel glared at me like it was my fault. "Sure, she called me the same way the other two did, and gave me the same kind of story. But I was getting to be a little smarter by then, because I'd been talking to Linda." He looked at the lieutenant again. "When I'd cooled off after visiting with Linda I realized just one thing; I was in love with her—I'd always loved her—but I hadn't been smart enough to know it. So I started seeing her again whenever I could, which wasn't often. That Marco bitch was always hovering around her. Linda swore she never called me in Chicago and I believed her, so it had to be somebody else who faked her voice."

"Ah, come on!" Santana said wearily.

"Somebody who hated the both of us," Sam persisted, "and figured to even the score."

"Oh, sure," Santana sneered. "Anybody could have faked her voice—and the voices of your other ex-wives! All they needed was to be a professional mimic, and have an intimate knowledge of your three marriages, plus an even more intimate knowledge of their sex lives after they were divorced."

"So all right, already," Sam said in a defeated voice, "I don't know from nothing! But I know I loved Linda, and if you figure I killed her you've got to be out of your tiny mind." He blinked rapidly. "She was the only woman for me; the only woman I've ever loved. You never even knew her, so how could you begin to understand her warmth, her beauty—"

"Why don't you get the hell out of here?" Santana suggested coldly. "We'll talk again in the morning."

Sorel got onto his feet and walked slowly out of the office. The lieutenant sighed deeply as the door closed, then pinched the bridge of his nose tight between his thumb and index finger.

"There are times," he muttered, "when I figure I'd like a nice clean job someplace, like working down a sewer!"

"How did he get to know the intimate details of their sex lives after divorce if those three dames didn't call him?" I asked. "Or somebody faking their voices didn't call him?"

"How the hell would I know? Maybe he hired some degenerate snooper, like you, to find out?"

"You can check that," I said.

"Thanks a bunch for reminding me!" His eyes glittered nastily. "What are you bucking for—my job?"

"I was just trying to help," I said modestly.

"Who? Your client?" He picked up the threatening letters from the desk and stuffed them into his inside coat pocket. "If he figured on killing her, he could have made up the letters and mailed them to himself. Then hired you to protect him from a mythical killer—one of his ex-wives—who never existed!"

"Maybe what we need right here is a couple of hard facts instead of interesting suppositions," I suggested.

"So I'll go see the two surviving ex-wives in the morning," Santana growled. "But I've got a couple of facts already, Holman; like, by his own admission, your client was right there at the scene of the murder, and at the right time. You want to go home and sleep on that?"

I shrugged. "It sounds like a good idea. Good night, Lieutenant."

He waited until I reached the doorway. "Just one more thing, Holman. I still haven't forgotten the last time we tangled on a homicide case. You came up with a real neat answer and a couple of extra stiffs, all by yourself. I wrote that off as a coincidence. I wouldn't do the same thing a second time. If somebody starts taking your kind of operation apart, it's vulnerable. Remember that!"

"My kind of operation is aimed at seeing that justice is done to my client," I said, restraining myself from saluting while I said it.

"Sure sounds pretty!" He lit another cigarette, then sneered. "I'd like to hear you tell it to the commissioner sometime, and maybe you will soon."

"I'm entitled to work for my client so long as I don't get in your way, and you know it," I grunted.

"Right." He bared his teeth at me. "So don't get in my way, Holman, or I'll rip you into small pieces!"

There was a flip answer to that hovering on the tip of my tongue, but as I was already withholding vital evidence from him I figured this was no time to use it.

CHAPTER SIX

"Your friendly neighborhood rapist is visiting again," I said, and pushed past the open-mouthed Beverly Quillen before she had a chance to slam the door in my face.

"I'll call the police!" she sputtered.

"Do that!" I snarled. "Tell them where you were tonight, around the time Linda Galen was stabbed to death."

"What?" The color drained out of her face.

"Let's talk about it." I took her arm and propelled her into the vaguely Oriental living room.

She collapsed onto the couch and I kept on going until I reached the bar and made a couple of shock-sized drinks. On the way back to the couch I noted that the ankle-length Mandarin hostess gown she was wearing matched the decor of the room, and wondered why she would wear a hostess gown if she hadn't been playing hostess. She almost grabbed the drink out of my hand, and the color slowly came back into her face as she forced it down.

"That's on the level? You wouldn't joke about something like murder, Rick? Her deep-blue eyes darkened as they watched my face. "Linda Galen was murdered tonight?"

"Sure." I sat down beside her. "Didn't Roger Hugill tell you about it?"

"Why, no, he only—" Her mouth set tightly. "That's a trick question, I suppose?"

"You suppose right," I agreed, "and you told me he

was about to marry you until Sam shot off his big mouth. But Hugill didn't even recognize your name when I spoke to him."

"Roger is the nervous type," she said in a cool voice. "You—with your rudeness and the way you bust into people's apartments and houses—he would figure as trouble. So he'd want to check you out before he even gave you the time of day."

"Sam says he'd fallen in love with Linda all over again. She said she never called him and he figured maybe that was true; maybe somebody had faked her voice over the phone. So when somebody called, saying they were Beverly Quillen, he got smart and didn't follow it up. That makes you a liar, honey."

"Or Sam!" She sat up straight. "He was here that night and it happened like I told you. I clobbered him with the ashtray and put him into a cab."

"You know his personal manager, Sonia Mayer?"

"No."

"She's an old friend of Hugill's and, coincidentally, she and Sam are going to stay at his house in Brentwood for the next couple of weeks."

"I know about that. Roger told me."

"When?"

"Tonight. He called me right after you left his place."

"But he didn't tell you about Linda Galen being murdered?"

"No." She finished her drink, got up from the couch and walked over to the bar. "Maybe he didn't believe you. Or maybe he was scared how I would react." She made herself a fresh drink and brought it back to the couch. "Compared to Roger, a clam is a blabbermouth, especially if he thinks he might become involved in something undignified."

"Like murder?"

She nodded. "Like murder."

"How did you get to meet him in the first place?"

"At a party."

"Beverly," I said sadly, "you're a congenital liar, right?"

"It's just that you're a congenital disbeliever in the truth," she retorted.

"So you met at a party, fell in love, and he was going to marry you until Sam told him about your nympho affairs with a string of other guys?"

"You put it so delicately, Rick!" She grimaced. "But, well, I guess that's about it."

"What kind of a guy is Roger Hugill, anyway?"

"He's forty-one years old, six feet tall, brown hair, gray eyes, and a moustache."

"That's cute!" I snarled.

"He's very rich, very respectable, and very devious." She widened her eyes as she looked at me. "Is that better?"

"A little," I said. "Did he ever talk with you about Sonia Mayer?"

"A little." She sipped her drink. "I had the feeling he would have liked to develop a relationship there, but she didn't see it that way. And he admired her for pulling Sam up by his bootstraps."

"Where were you between eight and nine tonight?"

"Right here."

"Alone?"

"Alone."

"Nobody called?"

"Not that I remember." She leaned back against the couch and closed her eyes. "Linda Galen was killed during that time, I presume? So I don't have an alibi, Rick. Do you want to call the police now or finish your drink first?"

"You're sure Sam called you around six thirty tonight and told you about me?" I asked.

"I'm sure." She sounded irritated. "He was loaded, slurring his words—the same old Sam-the-lush! Does it matter?"

"I don't know," I said truthfully. "Has Hugill ever been married?"

"Not that he ever told me. I don't think so." She opened her eyes again and gave me a long sideways glance. "I don't imagine you ever take advice, Rick?"

62

"Try me."

"Stay away from Roger. He eats people like you for an appetizer!"

"I figure he's some kind of a masochist," I said. "Who else would hang those dreadful bird pictures around the walls of his living room?"

"So he's got a peculiar taste in art." Her hand gripped my arm tight. "I'm serious about this, Rick. You don't know what kind of a man Roger is underneath that blustering exterior. I'll bet even money he has a two-inch-thick dossier on his desk by nine in the morning that tells the life history of one Rick Holman, from birth up until tonight, and doesn't omit one single detail!"

"Supplied by the Trushman Detective Agency?"

"I wouldn't know about that," she said quickly. "But if he thinks you're any kind of a threat to him after tonight, he'll stop at nothing to make sure you can't hurt him in any way."

"You sound like you're talking from personal experience."

She sighed heavily. "You're always reading something into a conversation that isn't there! Believe it or not, I'm only trying to help, Rick. With the money and influence Roger has in back of him he's got more power in his little finger than you'll ever have if you live to be a hundred, and he'll get luckier each year, too!"

I held my palm under her nose. "How about my future love life, seer?"

She knocked my hand away in an impatient gesture. "All right! See if I care when Roger cuts you down to a small boy!"

"Who hosted the party?"

"What the hell party was that?"

"The one where you first met Hugill."

"I don't remember." She drank some more liquor. "Yes, I do. A guy called Shelley; he was talking about giving me a job at the time, but it never did come to anything."

"What kind of job?"

"In plastics—Reynor Projects—they're a manufacturing outfit. He figured he could use a psychology

63

major in his personnel department. Most of the work in the plant was dull and routine, and because of it they had a big turnover in employees which was costing them money. But he finally went cold on the idea."

"How did you get to meet Shelley in the first place?"

"He called me one day—this was before I started work on the experimental psychology project at U.C.L.A. of course—and said he had this job in mind and was I interested. He'd checked on my qualifications and background and figured I was the right kind of person for the job. We had a couple of interviews, then he invited me to this party. I figured it was all part of the job-checking system, you know? He wanted to see how I behaved at a social function and all that idiotic jazz. Maybe that was where I flunked the test. From the time we were introduced, Roger monopolized me for the rest of the evening, and Shelley didn't approve. Anyway, I don't think I could have fallen in love with a plastics plant, or the people pushing all those buttons to produce ersatz chamber pots, or whatever the plastic gismo is that goes over big in the joke shops these days."

"If you'd gotten the job you wouldn't have had the chance to try your experimental psychology on me earlier tonight," I said.

She smiled reluctantly. "When I stripped down to a bra and panties, then threw myself at you? Right after you left I had the nasty suspicion that you'd one-upped me in the use of experimental psychology. That big reaction of yours was only to find out if I was kidding, right?"

"Never underestimate your enemy," I said.

"Or friend!" A questioning look came into her eyes. "What are you, Rick? My friend or enemy?"

"I haven't figured that out yet," I told her. "Maybe it's a little early in the relationship."

"I like you. Maybe you like me. Can't we just leave it like that for now?"

She got up from the couch and walked across to the bar again. But this time she left her empty glass right there and turned to face me. The hostess gown, which fitted her so modestly from neck to ankles, had a zipper down the front. She unzipped it all the way down to a point well below her midriff. Her eyes glowed with a deepening warmth as she looked at me, then she nuzzled her lower lip between her teeth for a moment.

"I'm depressed about Linda Galen having been murdered," she said in a low voice. "Even though I never knew her, we did kind of share the same husband at different times, and that brings her death close to me. I'm also tired, and right now I feel I'm about the loneliest woman in the whole wide world." She smiled, and the warmth in her eyes sparked into a kind of smoldering flame. "I think you're a nice guy, Rick, and we can make out in the sack together real good. How about that? No strings—no nothing. Just a couple of lonely people giving a little comfort to each other."

"Almost any other time but now I'd say it was a great idea," I told her. "But this is the wrong time, Beverly, and I'm in the wrong mood. I'm sorry, and I know I'll be a hell of a lot more sorry five minutes after I've walked out of here!"

She shrugged her arms out of the sleeves of the hostess gown, then let it drop into a soft heap around her ankles. She wasn't wearing anything underneath. There were two contrasting white horizontal stripes across her tanned body. I looked at the small, well-rounded breasts, the lean but firmly fleshed hips, and the graceful taper of her long legs, while I felt the desire rising inside me.

"You're sure you won't change your mind?" she asked in a throaty whisper.

"I'm sure," I muttered, "but don't think it's been easy." Then I forced myself onto my feet and headed toward the door.

"Well"—her dry chuckle pursued me into the front hall—"I guess it isn't every day a girl gets the chance to prove she's a natural redhead."

My watch said it was only a couple of minutes to two A.M. when I reached the car, and I figured it was almost time to call it a night—after I made one more stop. On the drive to the hotel I reflected it hadn't been too tough to resist Beverly Quillen's offer of bed and bawd. The way she had put it was more like a handout, and I didn't exactly relish the thought of playing some kind of a sexual panhandler. Maybe there will come a time but, I sincerely hoped, not before I reached my nonagenarian days.

It cost me plenty to get the bellhop to sneak me the passkey to Sam Sorel's room, not counting the best story I've dreamed up in a month. I hoped Sam wouldn't quibble about the extra expense.

I could have saved the tip and just knocked on the door, of course, but I figured that would rouse the beautiful blonde watchdog and I still wouldn't get to see Sorel. I figured he'd be asleep now, and if I was lucky I'd be in time for one of his nightmares.

I made the fifth floor by way of the back stairs and found room 505 without even stirring the dust on the beige carpet that was supposed to make the corridor look like a passageway to a room worth a million bucks but was five years too old to succeed.

The lock made a little click as I turned the key; then I pushed the door open soundlessly. Maybe I wasn't surprised at what I saw, but I hadn't expected it.

Sorel was asleep all right, but he wasn't alone. His personal manager had sat up to rock him to sleep. Her blouse open, revealing the fullness of her breasts, she sat with her back against the headboard, quietly stroking his head.

She looked up at me and smiled faintly. "How did you get a key, Rick?"

"Bribed a guy for it."

"Well, what do you want?"

"I wanted to talk to Sam." The door clicked behind me and I wandered over to the edge of the bed and stood there feeling that maybe I looked a little stupid.

"I'm sure Sam wouldn't know the answer to any of your questions this time of night, Rick." She kept on stroking his head but looking at me all the time.

"I thought I could find out whether or not he told

Santana the whole truth if you weren't around to protect him from the hard knocks."

"Very funny, Rick," she said levelly. "But I *am* around to protect him, day and night. Please understand that. And now get out of here and we'll see you tomorrrow."

I shrugged. "What's your version then? Is he a big, tough man who slugs women, beneath that exterior of soppy self-pity? Did he maybe write those lettters himself, for an excuse to—"

Her eyes flamed at me like two forty-fives. "Don't even think that, Rick. Not for a minute. He hired you to save his life, and that's all you—"

Sam interrupted her with a high-pitched scream. It was unnerving. I jumped back from the bed like I'd been bitten by a snake, but Sonia was right on the job.

She leaned forward swiftly and stroked his face and whispered softly in his ear things I couldn't hear.

Sam screamed again and threshed his arms around, almost clipping her in the ear, and then he began to calm down. She kept on crooning to him and his face relaxed and he began to breathe gently again.

When I went out the door she didn't look up.

I was just putting my foot on the front porch when a voice called out from the darkness.

"Rick. Is that you?"

"It's me, Sonia," I called back, checking the sudden impulse to dive into the shrubbery as I recognized her voice.

"I'm sorry, Rick." She smiled anxiously at me as I came up onto the porch. "But I have to talk now. It won't wait until morning."

"How did you get here ahead of me?" I asked, confused. "Hire a jet?"

"Just a taxi," she said contritely. "But they're the next best thing to a plane at three A.M."

"Well, come on in and catch your breath," I offered.

I opened the front door, switched on the lights, then took her through to the living room. She was wearing

67

that knockout dress that came in two sexy tiers, and the tiny copper bell dangling from her earlobe tinkled gaily as she sat down on the couch. I went over to the bar and busied myself with bottles, then carried the drinks over to the couch. "How's Sam?" I asked as I sat down beside her.

"Sleeping. I gave him enough Nembutal to knock over a large horse."

"So what won't wait until morning?" I asked. "That was your suggestion, remember?"

"You heard all those horrible things the lieutenant said to Sam tonight! And you must have believed them! As soon as you left, I began to think that you must think Sam has done something—well, something terrible." Sequins twinkled at me as the tier of lace over the bare swell of her full breasts fluttered gently. "I thought you were on Sam's side."

"Not if he murdered Linda Galen tonight."

"You simply *can't* believe that."

"Santana is almost believing it right now," I said. "Sam admits he was there around the time of the murder, and there's an eyewitness, too. The murder weapon was in the kitchen drawer for anybody to use. If Andrea Marco swears Linda wasn't about to leave her and go back to Sam, that would give him a strong motive for killing her. How do you think it would sound in court when she repeats the story of his first visit and what he did to Linda then? Jackie Slater can give a wonderful follow-up story of what happened when he visited with her, too!"

"But Sam didn't kill her, Rick. He couldn't!"

"Faith isn't proof, honey," I said, obviously.

"You have to help him, Rick!" Her eyes glowed with dedication. "He needs you more than ever right now."

"I'll try, but it won't be easy, having to do a soft-shoe shuffle around Santana the whole time."

She smiled warmly. "I knew you would. Thank you, Rick."

"If Sam didn't kill her—who did?"

"That Marco girl, of course," she answered promptly. "She'd do anything to stop Linda from going back to Sam."

"How about you?"

"Me?" She blinked. "You're not serious?"

"Where were you between eight and nine last night?"

"You are serious!" The warmth went out of her eyes and her voice became impersonal. "I had a meeting with Peter Aginos over at Stellar Productions this afternoon—a little horse-trading on the fine print clauses of Sam's contract—and we didn't finish up until after six. We had a couple of drinks afterward at the Wilshire; I guess it was around seven when I left there and went back to the hotel."

"What time did you get there?"

"Seven fifteen, about." She finished her drink and put the glass down carefully on the arm of the couch. "But then I went out again."

"Where?"

"Looking for Sam. It worried me when I found he'd gone out an hour before. So I went looking for him."

"You found him?"

She shook her head. "It was after eight when I got back to the hotel, maybe eight thirty or later—I don't remember—anyway, Sam came in soon afterward."

"So you don't have any alibi for the time of the murder?"

"I guess that's right." She nodded gravely. "Why do you think I killed Linda Galen, Rick?"

"You didn't want her coming back to Sam anymore than Andrea Marco did," I said. "Like you said earlier tonight, it's not so much a job but a lifetime of dedication. It wouldn't be the same at all with Sam married to another woman, would it?"

"No, it wouldn't." Her voice was flat. "Are you going to tell the lieutenant all this?"

"Roger Hugill," I said, ignoring her question. "Have you ever talked with him about Sam's ex-wives?"

"Not that I recall. Why?"

"You never mentioned Beverly Quillen to him?"

"I don't think so." Her eyebrows knit gently. "What has Roger got to do with me being your prime suspect?"

69

"Don't flatter yourself, Sonia," I told her. "You still only rate second to Sam. Were you and Hugill lovers at any time? Before Sam came into your life, I mean."

"No." She smiled slowly. "I think Roger had something like that in mind at the beginning, but I talked him out of it."

"Was that all it took? Just some talk?"

"Well, maybe something more than that. Roger is a very determined man, but I finally persuaded him to quit trying. Do you have any more personal questions to throw at me?"

"Are you and Sam lovers?"

"I love Sam, but we're not lovers. I told you before you'd never understand our relationship, Rick." Her eyes were tranquil and she looked directly at me. "But now—if it will make you work to get Sam out of this mess—I'll become your lover."

It was the second backhanded offer of the night, and I liked it even less than the first one. But I figured it might be interesting to find out just how much sincerity was behind it.

"Okay," I said harshly. "So take off your clothes and we'll go to bed."

"Here?"

"Sure," I nodded. "I get a kick out of watching big blondes strip in my living room!"

She sat motionless for what seemed like a long while, then the tears welled from her eyes and ran down her cheeks. I watched as she got up from the couch, then turned around to face me, her hands reaching for the zipper at the back of her dress.

"You would, too!" I said softly. "Anything for Sam, huh?"

"Isn't that what you want?" Her voice was brittle.

"I just changed my mind," I said. "I already have three big blondes on order, and five is a crowd in any bed."

"Thank you, Rick," she whispered, then turned around and walked out of the room.

I finished my drink as I listened to the sound of the front door close behind her. For a minute I thought about offering to drive her home, but what did I have against taxi drivers that I should spoil their nights? I spent a couple of uneasy minutes wondering just who, exactly, had proved a point back there, and wound up with the nasty feeling it hadn't been me.

CHAPTER SEVEN

Mr. Barre fitted real well into the nice solid background of the Trushman Detective Agency. He was a conservative dresser, smoked a pipe, and disdained to use a hairpiece to bolster his receding hairline.

The office itself was just as conservative in its style, and had that expensive look which transcends concern over making an impression. There was a thick gray carpet, a square, dark desk with a leather top, and a photograph of President Nixon on the wall.

"Pleasure to meet you, Mr. Holman," Barre said after we had been through the handshaking ritual, and he was safely established in back of his leather-topped desk. "I know you occasionally hire one of our operatives and"—his blue eyes twinkled knowingly—"I do have some appreciation of the status of your own clients, also your reputation for achievement. How can I help you?"

"I have a client right now," I told him. "Sam Sorel."

"Oh, yes?" His eyebrows lifted a fraction but that only proved he had read his morning newspaper.

"Sam is the marrying kind," I said. "Left a trail of three ex-wives behind him, and one of them was murdered last night. I wouldn't want to waste your time, Mr. Barre, so I'll come straight to the point. A few months back somebody hired your agency to run a check on his ex-wives; their addresses—activities—and especially their private lives. I'd like to see a copy of that report, and hear the name of the client who paid for it."

He carefully tamped down the tobacco in his pipe, then lit a match and let it burn down between his thumb and index finger. "I don't recall any such report from memory, Mr. Holman, but I'll surely check it out. Excuse me, please."

I lit a cigarette after he left the office and kept my fingers crossed. The whole deal was only a hunch, but I figured it was a logical one. The idea of all three ex-wives getting together in a murder conspiracy after each one had called Sorel and deliberately taunted him with the intimate details of her current sex life—just to make him real mad at them—was too fantastic. I was inclined to go along with Sam's theory that someone must have faked their voices when they called him. But whoever had done that first needed an expert knowledge of their private lives, and what better place to go for that than the Trushman Detective Agency?

Barre came back into the office and settled himself down in back of his desk with a regretful smile on his face. "No trace at all, I'm afraid. Perhaps someone quoted our name in error. Or even deliberately gave you a wrong steer. I know how often that can happen in our line of work!"

"And how is Mr. Hugill these days?" I asked warmly.

"Mr. Hugill?" His voice was very bland. "I don't think I understand."

"Your silent partner, Hugill," I said. "Who is also a friend of my client, and my client's personal manager, Sonia Mayer."

"Oh? Is that a fact?" He lit another match, then forgot to pick up his pipe.

"Lieutenant Santana is in charge of the homicide investigation," I said. "If I tell him the chances are you have a confidential report on Sorel's ex-wives kicking around this office, he'll be right down to check it out." I shook my head sadly. "That Santana! The original man from Missouri. He won't just take your word for it, Mr. Barre." I shrugged sympathetically. "But then you wouldn't want any trouble with the police, I guess?"

He knocked the fresh tobacco out of his pipe into a brass ashtray and started filling it again with more fresh tobacco. If the concept of the wasteful society appealed to him, his face didn't show it. Then he cleared his throat gently. "Roger said if you showed up at this office it would prove you were not quite the . . . uh . . . moron he thought you were last night. He also said he would see you at eleven tonight, at his house."

"That's real big of him, making time for a moron like me," I growled. "You mind if I use your phone and call the lieutenant now?"

"Give me a couple of minutes first, please." He opened the top drawer of his desk, took out a folder and carefully placed it in front of him. "This is a report from one of our top operatives—you could say he's a genius at tailing people. Some of our other operatives claim he's found the secret of invisibility. I think that's exaggerated, of course, but not very much." He opened the folder and leafed through the first couple of pages. "Here it is. I'll keep it down to the essential details: Subject left restaurant at 8:10 P.M. Drove to West Hollywood—and so on. Entered apartment building through service area at rear at 8:28 P.M. Subject left building the same way at 8:42 P.M." He closed the folder and gave me a brief commiserating smile. "All the details are there, Mr. Holman. Do you still wish to call Lieutenant Santana?"

"You had one of your operatives tailing me last night?" I almost choked as the realization hit me. "And I didn't spot him!"

"Like I said," Barre tried real hard not to look smug, "he's a near genius when it comes to keeping tabs on people. Naturally, he knew your reputation before he took the assignment. I understand he regarded it as quite a challenge."

There was no point in trying to wipe the egg off my face because it was going to stick for a long time. "So now we've got a Mexican standoff?" I grated. "If I tell Santana about the report on Sorel's ex-wives, you'll make sure you show him your operative's reports on my movements last night?"

"Something like that, I imagine."

"I figure you should introduce me to your genius operative," I said bitterly. "We can travel in the same car and save his expenses, now that I know he'll be around the whole time."

"You'll know he's there—if you see him. Maybe—just maybe—Roger won't find his services necessary now."

"You mean now that he's gotten something on me!"

He nodded placidly. "On the other hand, don't get careless. I'm sure you have more than one sin that can be discovered."

"Pay me ten cents an item and I'll tell you the list," I growled. "Well, it hasn't been fun talking with you, Mr. Barre."

"I have to admit *I've* enjoyed our little chat, Mr. Holman." This time he actually lit his pipe and puffed away contentedly. "It isn't often Roger lets me in on a little of his fun and games."

I went out of the Trushman offices and straight to the nearest bar, in need of a cushion to absorb the mortifying shock. If I got any more shocks like that it would be time to look for a different line of work, like maybe playing stooge to some comic in a girlie show. It was about time for lunch but Trushman's genius operative had destroyed my appetite, so I decided to go visit with my unfavorite blonde instead.

When I got there nobody answered the doorbell. I rang it for about three minutes repeatedly, then remembered her brother lived directly across the hall. On my third ring, the door opened a whole five inches, with the chain still hooked. Frank Marco squinted at me suspiciously through the opening.

"Holman," I snapped. "I was there in the office with the lieutenant last night."

"Oh, yes!" He unhooked the chain and opened the door wide. "Come in, Mr. Holman." He closed the door quickly and hooked the chain back into place. "I thought it was probably another one of those dreadful reporters. They've been making life completely impossible for us ever since the very crack of dawn."

"I want to talk with your sister," I said.

He fingered his cut and swollen lower lip in a quick nervous reaction. "Poor Andrea is still terribly upset about the ghastly murder. I don't think the poor darling slept a wink last night after we got back. Of course I absolutely insisted she should stay here with me." The dramatic shudder set all his fat gently quivering. "Well, I mean, can you imagine living in an apartment after your dearest friend has just been murdered there? It would be simply too ghoulish!"

"Your sister?" I repeated impatiently.

"In the living room, Mr. Holman. Please be gentle with her." His watery blue eyes blinked rapidly. "She isn't . . . well . . . she isn't quite herself at the moment, if you understand me."

"Sure," I grated. "I'm the original velvet-gloved kid. Now can we go see her?"

The living room had an old hat high camp look to it—the way Frank Marco did—and the hanging mobile of little colored glass balls was a listless antique from before the time the flower generation came and went. Andrea Marco was sitting on a couch covered with Thai silk that was scuffed and a hideous not-quite-purple color. She was wearing an ankle-length black silk robe that could have made her a pallbearer, except she obviously didn't have the strength for it right then. Her long blond hair hung down below her shoulders and all the luster seemed to have vanished from it. Only the black-rimmed eyes burning in her pale face were alive.

"Get out!" she said in a low venomous whisper.

"Just one question," I said.

"You fingered her for Sorel yesterday and I'll never forgive you for that, Holman."

"Now, Andrea, honey!" Her brother's high-pitched voice sounded shaky. "You don't know that's true at all."

The look she gave him would have made a Borgia blanch. He took a quick involuntary step backward and nearly tripped over a fake camel saddle that badly needed a new paint job. "All right, Sis, whatever you say!" He ran his hands through his long blond hair in a theatrical gesture of despair, then looked like he was about to burst into tears.

I concentrated on Andrea again. "Did you, or Linda, ever know a guy called Hugill?"

"I told you to get the hell out of here!"

"Answer the question and I'll go," I told her.

"Hugill?" She shook her head briefly. "I never heard the name before."

"A tall guy, around forty," I persisted. "Brown hair and a bristling moustache. Kind of gives you the impression that if he'd been with Custer the Indians would have surrendered."

"There was a man who looked like that." She thought about it for a couple of seconds. "He came into the boutique almost every day for a while and he always wanted Linda to look after him. It got so that every time she saw him coming, she'd duck into the back room and ask me to front for her—say she was sick, or something. After that happened a few times he lost interest, I guess, because he stopped coming into the boutique."

"When was that?" I asked.

"A few months back, I don't remember exactly." Her lower lip curled. "Are you going to try and prove that man killed Linda?" She gave a short derisive laugh and I shuddered at the sound of it. "We all know who killed her, Holman. It was Sorel, and I'm going to make very sure he suffers for it! Sorel is a—" She started mumbling a long string or unoriginal obscenities.

"Sis!" Marco shrilled. "That isn't nice! A girl with your background just shouldn't talk that way."

Surprisingly, she stopped, laid her head back against the couch, and closed her eyes. "Get me a drink!"

"Right away, Sis," Marco said happily. "How about you, Mr. Holman? Would you care for a glass of dry sherry?"

I winced. "Sounds great."

He disappeared into the kitchen and came back carrying an op-art tray with three dinky little glasses of

77

straw-colored sherry clattering away to themselves happily. Andrea opened her eyes and sat up, then took a glass from the tray. Her eyes focused on me and started to burn again.

"What the hell is Holman still doing here? I told him to get out!"

"Now, Sis." Marco made a placating gesture with his free hand. "Mr. Holman is only trying to help."

"Help Sorel, you mean." She sipped her drink, grimaced sharply, then hurled the glass across the room. "What the hell are you doing, giving me that mouthwash to drink! I want a martini!"

Marco went down on his hands and knees to pick up the pieces of the shattered glass. When he stood up again his face was contorted with anger. "How could you, Andrea! You know they're my very favorite glasses. Imported Swedish, too, and they can't be replaced!"

"Stop whining, and get me that martini," she snarled.

"I won't!" He stamped his foot, and I wouldn't have believed it if I hadn't seen it. "I won't! Get it yourself!"

She got up from the couch with a disdainful sneer fixed on her face and walked stiffly into the kitchen. I just hoped she'd bring two martinis back with her, but it was wishful thinking and I knew it.

Marco edged close toward me in a kind of furtive shuffle that made me feel real nervous for a moment. "I know Andrea's emotionally disturbed," he confided in a whisper, "but I do think she's carrying on a little too much! The shock of Linda having been murdered, and then finding the body. I mean, I can understand all that and I do sympathize with the poor girl. But all these dreadful melodramatics are beginning to get me down. Smashing one of my favorite glasses was purely malicious, Mr. Holman. Even though I do say it about my own sister, it was purely malicious! After all, it's not as if their relationship was going to last forever, is it?"

"How's that again?" I queried.

"She and Linda." He shrugged his shoulders expressively. "It would have been all over in another month at most. Linda was definitely going back to Sorel, I know it." He raised his eyes toward the ceiling and shook his head wonderingly. "The dreadful fights those girls had! Some of them had to be seen to be believed, I assure you."

"But Linda only saw him the one time when he crashed into her apartment about three months back. Leastwise, that's what your sister told the lieutenant last night."

"Pride." He pursed his soft lips together and his voice became unctuous. "She lied because she couldn't take the truth. Linda had been seeing Sorel at every opportunity, and there weren't that many opportunities with Andrea watching her like a mother hen the whole time. But it was all building to a climax. That's why I stopped Sorel from going into her apartment last night. I thought he'd come to take Linda away with him, and I knew if I let it happen Andrea would make all kinds of hell for me when she found out." His voice had climbed back to its normal level as he talked. "I guess you have some idea by now, Mr. Holman, of just how hard to live with my sister can be at times."

"At it again, brother?" Andrea said from the open kitchen doorway. "Exchanging little confidences about me behind my back?"

She walked over to the couch and sat down. The color drained out of Marco's face as he watched her sip her martini. I tasted the pale sherry and suppressed a shudder. So maybe it was a great sherry but how could a confirmed bourbon drinker tell?

"I was only saying you'll have to face up to reality sooner or later, Sis," Marco said in a strangled voice. "That's all."

"Just what kind of reality is that?" she asked.

"Well"—he was betrayed by his own big mouth and knew it—"I mean, your life with Linda wouldn't have lasted forever, would it?"

"Why not?"

Marco gestured helplessly. "She would have gone back to Sorel."

"I wouldn't insult my mother's memory by calling you a lying son of a bitch! Linda never wanted any part of Sorel!" She spat the words at him. "She was scared of him, that's all. You were supposed to protect the both of us from him, but you don't have the guts of a sparrow. Can't you get it through your thick skull that Linda loved me? She would have always loved me, you spineless cretin! Why else do you think Sorel killed her?"

"It's not true!" A faint note of hysteria crept into his voice. "You know, inside, that it's not true. She was ready to walk out on you with Sorel and marry him again, only you don't want to think about it now she's dead!"

"It was me she loved." The way Andrea said it, it was a flat dogmatic statement of conviction. "Nothing could ever change that while she lived."

"Sis—" Marco blinked the tears out of his eyes, then stumbled across to the couch and went down on his knees beside her. "Don't say that," he whimpered. "Please!"

I saw the look of absolute loathing on her face as her brother buried his head in her lap, and figured it was about time for Holman to depart. You don't get to meet many normal people in my line of work, but at least most of them are never dull. I started toward the door, leaving the nearly full sherry glass on the table.

"Sis—" Marco's voice was muffled, so he sounded like a small boy pleading for his heart's desire. "*Please?*"

I heard her voice reply just as I reached the front hall and my spine froze as the impact of her words hit me.

"You poor, stupid, fool!" Her tone of voice was a mixture of incredulity and contempt. "You can't be thinking that now—just because Linda is dead—I would ever come back to your arms?"

After the jolt I had just gotten at Marco's apartment, I decided I needed a short drive to clear my head. And after a couple of blocks, I remembered the previous shock handed out to me at the Trushman Detective Agency.

It took me three miles of driving straight down Santa Monica Boulevard before I began to catch on to the trick. The same trick that every nine-year-old kid with a magic kit learns before he even waves a wand. Make them look where you want them to.

Naturally, I was looking behind me. But the thin man with the crew cut and the bushy moustache, wearing a golf cap and driving the cream Jag with a Los Angeles Rams sticker on the left batwing, was in front of me.

He was smart all right. He used reverse psychology as well: If you want to hide from someone who's looking for you, be as conspicuous as hell.

I caught on because I was only doing twenty, yet for two miles I never lost sight of him. No guy who runs a Jag pedals along at twenty miles an hour on a hot, cloying, smog-filled summer morning, when in twenty minutes he could be where the birds and the breeze are.

I speeded up, but even a Thunderbird with a herd of horses neighing beneath the hood is restrained from free expression in the heart of L.A. traffic. It wasn't heavy, and you could do a good forty, stopping and starting between bursts, but there wasn't any hope of getting closer to the Jag than Andy Capp wanted me to.

I could have played around with him all morning but there didn't seem to be any point to it.

The spot I picked out for our meeting wasn't elegant, but it was rich. On Signal Hill the squat pumps suck the oil out of the ground like beetles with their proboscises sunk into the earth. There are thousands of the little monsters, working tirelessly with a mechanical precision that would have made Errol Flynn envious. Some have tall, erector-set derricks squatting over them, others do not, and they spread over the area the way locusts blanket a wheat field.

The instant I parked the car I was running. I wanted to get away from the road before he spotted me. I had parked on the crest of a hill and he was about a quarter of a mile behind me, so I knew I could make it.

I crouched behind a corrugated iron shed used by maintenance men and waited for the sound of his engine to slow and stop.

He came up the slope fast and over the crest of the hill. His toe didn't even twitch on the accelerator and if I had been waiting for him in the car he would probably have smiled and waved his hand, a friendly fellow sportster on the road to nowhere.

I waited. The roar of the powerful engine faded into the distance. As far as I could tell, he didn't stop. But I gave him more credit than that.

I took off through the oil field. It was like running through a putrified forest in a witch's dream. The insects raised and lowered their heads in monotonous time to the dirge of the faint, far-off wind that whipped through the tops of the steel towers.

When I spotted him I had to stop and suck in some breath. Along with the bobbing monsters, I breathed in the petroleum stench of long-dead animals, filling up my lungs with the gaseous effluvium of man's acquisitive nature.

Andy had his cap off now. He had thrown it rakishly on the point of his radio antenna. The soft gray mold of his head made him look like a bald walrus. He was standing on top of a hill above the road.

I figured he could see my car through the binoculars he was holding to his eyes.

I made a wide circuit and crossed the road around a bend. Then I came up behind him. I was still twenty feet away when he lowered the binoculars and, without turning around, said, "Don't come any closer, Mr. Holman."

My revolver was in my hand before he'd finished the sentence, but I felt like a man with a pair of aces playing against a stacked deck.

Still with his back turned, as if he had radar beneath that round, rocklike dome beeping waves from his sonar ears, Andy said: "Put the gun away, stupid. This is real-life cops and robbers, not vintage Sam Spade."

I stood looking at his broad back. He was wearing

a wine-colored sports shirt. Cotton, but expensive. It was tucked into an ordinary pair of white ducks. Clean, put on this morning. Underneath his arms the wine was stained by his sweat. He wore golf sneakers and put a lot of weight into them. He was a big man and I was perfectly willing to concede that he was tough. His clothes weren't filled out with fat.

"You sweat," I said. "It's not fashionable."

"The girls tell me it's sexy," he said. "But I guess a slicked up pretty-boy like you wouldn't know about real women, right, Holman?" His rough-edged voice handled my name as if it were an obscene word.

"I'm sorry you said that," I growled. "I was hoping we were going to be friends."

"Let's face it," he said evenly, "that gun makes you look sillier than you sound." His lower lip was wide and fleshy. When he smiled it folded over until it almost touched his chin. "Point 1: I'm a private, licensed cop. Point 2: I'm out on a harmless jaunt of my own, doing a little bird-watching, when I'm attacked by a punk who thinks his license entitles him to wave revolvers in front of people. Point 3: Talk your way out of it, smart boy."

What was the point in arguing? I slipped the gun inside my coat. "The only birds you'd find around here would be vultures," I pointed out.

"Thanks," he said, almost pleasantly. "Guns make me nervous."

"Now that we're on speaking terms, you can tell me how you like working for Roger Hugill."

"Never heard of him."

"You've heard of him."

"So I'm loyal."

"Ever heard of Sam Sorel? Hugill have you shadowing him too?"

The big man licked his lips with a fat tongue, then tasted the tips of his moustache. "Listen, Holman, ask me if I've heard of Walt Disney and I'd tell you what I just told you: Never heard of him. You should understand a man in my position can't go blabbing his mouth off."

"How about as a personal favor to me?"

"As a personal favor I wouldn't lick a stamp for you if you were dying of thirst. Get lost."

"I guess you just won't be friendly, no matter how hard I try," I snapped as I drew out the gun again. Billy the Kid could have laid me out before I got my finger on the trigger, but I was quick enough to surprise Andy.

With the suddenness of a summer shower, his smile disappeared. There was a hard, cold look in his gray eyes. "You're playing with guns again, Holman. I don't like it."

I nodded. I understood how he felt, but it wasn't my fault if he let little things upset him.

His car was about forty feet downhill. I aimed and fired, hitting the right front tire, then leveled the barrel back at him.

"You'll need a big patch for that one," I said.

He said nothing but it was easy to see I'd made him unhappy.

"That your car?" I asked.

Still nothing.

"Give me a couple of answers, and I'll spare the body beautiful."

"Listen, Holman. You shoot up that car and I'll—"

"Did you shadow Sam Sorel for Hugill?"

"Yeah."

"Were you behind him the night he beat up Linda Galen?"

"If he ever beat up anybody I don't know about it."

I thought about that for a minute while I watched him, wishing he'd slugged me before I got the drop on him again.

"You don't know, but maybe he could have?"

"Maybe."

"Did he ever visit Beverly Quillen while you were tagging him?"

"Nope."

I gave him my hard stare, just to let him know I didn't believe a word he'd said, and then I blew the left rear tire.

He jumped at that one. "You lousy bastard!"

"Tell me," I said. "Why do you do jobs for Hugill? And don't tell me you don't know what kind of a rat he is."

"Never heard of the man."

I figured I was wasting my time, so I left him there and went back to my car. It was a hot day, too hot to be fixing flat tires, but I didn't feel too sorry for old Andy. After all, he wasn't exactly sociable.

CHAPTER EIGHT

Graham was sitting in the manager's office, formally dressed this time in a neat blue suit and conservative tie. It was his night to go visit with his mother, I remembered. He smiled uncertainly when he saw me and I preferred to think it was in welcome.

"Hello there, Rick." The grin got a little twisted. "You're early. I don't leave until around five thirty, but no hard feelings."

"Is Jackie home?" I asked.

He shrugged. "I wouldn't know for sure, I haven't seen her anytime today. Why don't you go find out?"

"It's a thought," I agreed. "I wanted to ask you something first. You told me she had a regular gentleman caller who used to sneak in on Tuesday nights, remember? What did he look like?"

"How the hell would I know? I visit with my mother on—"

"Sure, sure!" I grated. "But how the hell did you know he existed if you never saw him?"

"Traces," he said, then grinned when I stared at him blankly. "You know? The cigar butt in the trash can, the new bottle of liquor on the shelf. I'm a very observant guy, Rick, especially when it comes to two-timing dames. When I felt real sure, I tossed it at her one night. She admitted it was true, but then she clammed up and wouldn't tell me one single thing about the guy. My theory is it was Batman and she didn't want to make Robin jealous."

"I guess I'll go see if she's home," I said.

"Let me extend the courtesy of the motor court and call her room." He got up from the desk and walked into the small side room where, I cleverly guessed, the switchboard was housed. Around thirty seconds later he returned and shook his head. "You're out of luck, Rick. I let it ring long enough to get her out of the shower, even, but there's no answer. If Jackie's home she always answers the phone because she figures it could be her big chance calling."

"And so it was," I told him. "I was just about to offer the leading role in a new blockbuster called *Sorel and Me*."

"She was going to play Me?"

"Sorel," I corrected him. "I figure she knows Sam better than he knows himself. In fact, I'm rapidly coming to the conclusion that almost anybody knows Sam better than he knows himself."

"This is a tough one, huh, Rick?" His voice oozed with the kind of respectful sympathy that was an open invitation for me to confide in him.

While that Trushman operative had been tailing me all over town I hadn't even known it. No intuitive feeling, no short hairs bristling at the nape of my neck. But now I had a feeling about Graham; that "traces" bit had sounded a little too contrived, and how come he suddenly got generous and called her room instead of letting me walk over there to find out if she was home, like he was going to do in the first place?

"It's tough, okay," I said. "But I have a kind of hunch about Jackie's gentleman caller." I checked my watch. "I'll come back in a couple of hours and see if she's home then. Give my regards to your mother, Harv."

I went back to the car, drove slowly around the block three times, then parked outside the motor court. The manager's office was empty when I snuck my head around the door, so I headed toward room number ten. When I got there, the front door was open maybe a couple of inches, like somebody had gone inside in a hurry. I listened and heard voices coming from inside, then a sharp slapping sound immediately followed by an anguished yelp. It looked like I had arrived in the nick of time, and all that jazz. Then I had a sudden vision of just how much those triceps expanded whenever Harv flexed them, and the hero drained out of me fast. From inside the room there was the sound of another sharp slap, followed by an even more anguished yelp. There was no choice but to push the door open wide and keep my fingers crossed that Harv didn't know how to fight dirty.

The starlet was a wondrous sight to behold; standing there in a black bra and the briefest briefs I had ever seen, consisting of a front and back panel of polka-dotted white silk, joined by two thin silken strips on each curve of her rounded hips. Both her cheeks flamed a blotchy red, which accounted for the slapping sounds I'd heard. Graham was facing her, his back toward me, as I came into the room.

"You'll keep your stupid mouth shut," he snarled. "You understand? You tell Holman nothing. In fact you won't be around when he comes back. Go out someplace for the night—any place—but stay out of his way."

"You cheap bastard!" she snarled back at him. "Who the hell do you think you are, treating me this way. I'll do what I goddamned well want to with Holman!"

"You tell him anything, baby," he said in a low voice, "and I'll fix your face so good, you'll get a nervous breakdown every time you look in a mirror!"

"But, Harv," I said reproachfully, "what would your mother say?"

He froze momentarily as I'd hoped he would. I clenched my hands together, pivoted on one foot, then let him have the double-fist in his right kidney with all my weight in back of the swing. For a terrifying moment nothing happened, then he sagged slowly onto his knees. Jackie Slater took the opportunity to prove she was the sporting type, and backhanded him across each side of his face. His head rocked a little but that was all. I moved around in front of him cautiously until I saw his face, then stopped worrying. His skin was a gray wasteland, and even the starlet's backhanders hadn't brought any color back into it. His jaw was set tight and his lips writhed back from his teeth in a fixed grimace of pain. I figured it would be a couple more minutes before he could do anything, and even then he'd probably only manage to scream a little. But he was still a minor problem because he obviously couldn't walk out of the room by himself, and it would have taken twin Holmans to toss him out.

"Jackie," I said to the silver-blonde, "how about putting on some clothes and we'll go have a drink someplace."

"Sure, Rick." She looked at me fondly. "You sure gave Harv his comeuppance!" Her eyelashes batted provocatively. "I bet you just don't know your own strength!"

"I know my own strength," I told her. "That's why I hit him from behind while he wasn't looking. How about those clothes?"

"Oh, sure!" There was a sudden thump as Graham pitched forward onto his face and lay stretched out on the floor. Before she headed toward the closet, Jackie climaxed the shining hour by kicking him in the ribs, stubbing her bare toes painfully in the process.

A couple of minutes later she was ready to face the world, wearing skintight canary-yellow pants and a patterned silk blouse basically the color of a tropical sunset. At the last moment she added the starlet's essential—the huge blue-framed sunglasses. L.A. had to be the only place in the world, I silently philosophized, where that kind of outfit ensured the wearer would blend into a crowd.

Graham let out a loud groan as we reached the doorway. I looked back over my shoulder and saw he was twitching a little; I figured he shouldn't have any trouble later in the night when his mother asked, "What's new?" A pulverized kidney would be good for an hour's monologue.

Simple deduction told me the best place for a quiet drink and chitchat with Jackie Slater was the Holman residence, so I drove straight home. When we got inside the house I headed toward the bar, while Jackie prowled around the living room inspecting both the furniture and the furnishings with such great interest she even removed her cheaters. Then, having completed the inspection, she dropped onto the couch and heaved a deep sigh.

"Well, that did up Harv real good, in the one creepy old package!"

"Are you pining?" I asked politely.

"For that cheap sonuvabitch?" She sniffed disparagingly. "It was just about over, anyway. But it finished right there, when he hit me."

I took myself and the drinks over to the couch, then sat down beside her. "Looks like he didn't want you talking to me about the guy who used to visit on Tuesday nights?"

"You should have seen the look on his face when you hit him!" She gave a gloating chuckle. *"Kerr-plunk!* And he looked like the sky had fallen in on his head. Then he went down on his knees like he was about to beg my forgiveness, only he couldn't even speak then!" She chuckled again. "And, boy! Did I let him have it! One—two! His little old head almost fell off his stupid shoulders!" Her lips pouted sorrowfully. "If I'd thought about it at the time I could have given him a swift kick in the—"

"Never mind!" I interrupted hastily. "Harv won't forget the both of us over the next few days. You know why he was so determined to stop you from telling me about the guy who used to visit on Tuesday nights?"

Her eyebrows knit over the Kewpie-doll blue eyes, then she tilted the glass to her lips and drained it in one practiced swallow. "I don't know, Rick," she said finally, "and I guess that's kind of strange, huh? I mean, Harv was supposed to be crazy jealous about the guy beating his time with me, so if you meant trouble for the guy it would figure the other way around. Like Harv would want me to tell you everything, not stay clammed up."

"The guy being Roger Hugill?" I said casually.

"Huh?" She gave me that blank look again, then pushed her empty glass into my hand. "Be a doll and made me a fresh drink. I've got this dreadful thirst, and my nerves are all shot after the way Harv slapped me around."

I wouldn't have minded being Harv right then, so I

could give her another slap in the teeth. Instead, I took the glass back to the bar and started making her a fresh drink.

"So it wasn't Hugill?" I asked in a wondering voice.

"Rick, honey." She gave me the full treatment: the big phony smile, the eyelashes batting a real high average, and the long, deep breath flattening her blouse. "I don't know how to say this exactly, but his name is kind of confidential. I mean, I'm not the kind of girl who does—then tells!"

"I understand." I gave her a real sunny smile, then let my face sober into a pallbearer's look, like right after somebody had just dropped the front end. "You know Linda Galen was murdered last night?"

"I read about it in the newspapers." Her eyes widened. "Isn't that awful?"

"The thing is," I said in a somber voice, "I figure she was only the first one to go!"

"How's that again?" She blinked. "The first what?"

"Ex-wife. I'm almost certain the killer is out to get the three of you, and Linda Galen was only the start." I shrugged helplessly. "Trouble is, nobody seems interested in helping me nail him before he kills again."

Her mouth opened and closed again a couple of times before she got the words out. "But that's horrible, Rick!" Her voice jumped a half octave. "You mean"—full realization hit and her voice jumped the other half octave—"he could be going to kill me?"

I gave her a slow, pitying smile. "If my hunch is right, Jackie, you're the next victim on his list. I don't know why, but it's always the same. Nobody wants to cooperate until it's too late."

She came off the couch like she'd just been goosed by somebody who wasn't in the movie business, then headed toward me at a quick run. A moment later she grabbed the freshly made drink from the bar and gulped it down like liquor was going out of style. "But you told me it was one of us ex-wives who was threatening to kill Sam. Why does he want to kill the three of us?" A look of horrified understanding showed up in her eyes. "The alimony! The lousy sonuvabitch wants to quit paying alimony and the only way out is to kill the—"

"Who the hell's talking about Sam?" I snarled.

"You were!" She bit down on her lower lip. "Weren't you?"

"Sam had fallen in love with Linda Galen all over again," I said. "He wanted to marry her for a second time, so why would he kill her? It's Hugill I'm talking about."

"Roger?" She pushed her empty glass toward me in a reflex gesture, and I wondered if it wouldn't be easier just to give her a fresh bottle with a couple of ice cubes on the side. "Roger!" She repeated the name and this time there was a dull ring of conviction in her voice. "He's psycho, huh? I always figured the guy was just kinky and—hell!—who isn't around these parts? But I can see it now."

"At long last you're cooperating!" I said. "Tell me everything you know about him, what happened between you, the works."

"Sure thing, Rick." She eyed her empty glass expectantly. "Be a doll and—"

"Later," I said firmly. "Let's hear the story first, while you're still coherent enough to tell it."

"Got a cigarette?" Her hands were trembling so much I had to hold the match for her. "Well, you know how it is in the movie business, Rick. When I got divorced from Sam it didn't make any difference to my career because he was right at the bottom of the heap, and people didn't even remember his name. But when he made that big comeback, it was different. All kinds of creeps started remembering I was one of his ex-wives and that sometime maybe they would want a favor from him. So they figured it wouldn't be smart to do one of his ex's any favors, especially like work! A couple of months back it had gotten so bad I was seriously thinking of doing away with myself!"

She held the dramatic pose with her eyes downcast, body slumped, and hands clasped loosely in front of her for around three seconds. Then she gave me a quick sideways glance for the reaction. I clapped my hands together three times, real slow.

"So all right, already!" Her voice became aloof. "But it *was* real bad, Rick! Then, one day out of the blue, I got a call from this Hugill character. He said he was putting up the money—around thirty percent of the budget—for a new movie starring Harvey Mountfort. They were looking for a second female lead and he'd heard a lot about my work. I figured it was just another come-on, so I told him to drop dead and hung up. He called right back and said he appreciated my reaction, but he was making a genuine offer and would I see him in his office."

"Which office was that?" I said, because I didn't want to spend the next forty-eight hours listening to her total recall.

"Wallace Productions. They're an independent outfit, Rick, and—"

"I know that," I rasped. "What I didn't know was Hugill had a piece of the outfit. So what happened then?"

"I saw him at his office and he was charming; talked about the movie, and even gave me the script to read. It finished up with him asking me out to dinner and I went, of course." Her eyelashes batted demurely at me. "Then—well—you know?"

"The two of you had a special relationship. So?"

"Everything seemed to be going just fine. Like I said before, he was a little kinky but nothing too way out. He used to ask a lot about Sam and what it was like being married to him. I figured he was just naturally curious. Then, suddenly, it was all over. He just didn't show up at the motor court anymore. When I called his office he was always out. After a couple of weeks of that, some creep in his office called me and said they were sorry but they'd found another actress for the part. I kept on asking myself, so what did our girl do wrong? Only I never came up with an answer. Hey!" She frowned deeply. "I just remembered something."

"Where you left your mind?" I grunted.

"Don't kid around, Rick, this could be important. The last time Roger visited was a few days after Sam had busted into the place and come on like the cheated husband, yet! I told Roger all about it, because with all those other questions he'd asked about Sam, I figured he'd be interested. You figure that could be the reason he dropped me like a dead fish afterward?"

"Maybe. Did Hugill know you were one of Sorel's ex's, or did you tell him?"

"Of course he knew," she said confidently. "He mentioned it that very first night, while we were having dinner."

"Did he ever mention either of the other two ex's?"

"I don't think so. I'm almost sure he didn't, Rick, but maybe he was just being tactful."

"More like devious." I made the fresh drink and pushed it across the bar. "You've been a big help, Jackie."

"I have?" She looked at me hopefully. "You figure you can nail him before he murders me?"

"I'm goddamned sure of it," I said confidently.

"So make yourself a drink and we'll celebrate." She leaned across the bar toward me, her eyes moist with promise. "Let's celebrate, honey. I want to show you the proper appreciation for saving my life."

"Only one small problem there, Jackie," I said carefully. "If I start celebrating right now, I won't have the time to go out and nail Hugill before he tries to murder you, right?"

"Right!" She straightened up fast. "Well? What the hell are you waiting for? Don't just stand there, get going!"

"A couple of minutes won't make any vital difference," I assured her. "I'll call a cab to take you home first."

"Home?" she exploded. "If you figure I'm about to go back to that motor court and chitchat with Harv, you've got to be out of your mind!" She shook her head determinedly. "I'm waiting right here until you get back and tell me Roger is locked up safe someplace."

"Okay," I said reluctantly. "But leave some of the liquor for when I get back, huh?"

I went into the bedroom, got the belt holster and the

thirty-eight out of the top bureau drawer, then put them on under my coat. Jackie Slater was curled up on the couch when I got back into the living room, her drink cradled in both hands.

"Good luck, Rick!" The lashes batted quickly, and the magnificent bosom heaved as she threw me a kiss like it was all I would ever need. "Hurry home. I'll be waiting, honey!" Her eyes told me all that would be waiting for me in sight-language words of one syllable.

"If it feels like you're floating," I said anxiously, "don't worry. They've never had a flood in Beverly Hills yet. Just don't try and make the bar. You'll be fine right there on the couch."

"You're just about the nicest man I know, Rick," she purred.

"That goes for me, too," I agreed.

"I wish there was a flood! So just the two of us could be marooned here together for weeks and weeks!"

"Well, don't make any waves!" I got out of the room fast; even if being assaulted by a starlet was a kind of nifty idea, it didn't fit in my schedule right then.

CHAPTER NINE

I stopped off at a drive-in for a couple of quick hamburgers and a cup of coffee on the way. It was only around eight when I arrived at the high-rise apartment.

Beverly Quillen opened the door and looked at me like I was some kind of a disaster area all by myself.

"Another evening ruined!" She shook her head despairingly. "What did I ever do to deserve you?"

"Got lucky, I guess?" I said quickly. "You want to ask me in, or do I have to shove you out of the way?"

"Oh, come in by all means." She waved her arms wildly. "Be my guest, Mr. Holman. Make yourself at home—eat off the floor—spill your drinks over the covers—see if I care!"

"You're still in your clothes and I've been here a full minute already." I looked at her doubtfully. "Am I losing my sex appeal or something?"

"You're a riot tonight," she said from between clenched teeth. "If there's any justice, one of these nights you're going to throw yourself at me. Then I'm going to duck at the last moment and watch you fly clean out the window!"

The redhead turned away abruptly and I followed her stiff, unyielding back into the living room. As soon as she reached the couch she spun around quickly and faced me with a determined look in her eyes.

"Don't bother to sit down, Rick," she said crisply.

"You won't be staying that long. So—whatever it is—make it brief."

She was wearing a white crepe dress that buttoned all the way down one side to the hemline, riding about four inches above her knees. The white lace stockings set off her shapely legs, and the square-toed shoes matched their color perfectly. Somehow, the outfit was just right for her tall slenderness; the all-whiteness emphasized the contrasting planes of her intelligent face and set fire to her titian hair.

"You're looking very elegant tonight, Beverly," I told her.

In spite of herself, she grinned faintly. "Well! That's something I never expected to hear from you. A compliment for an insatiable little old nympho like me?"

"If you're a nympho," I said, "then I'm a boy scout."

"You could have fooled me the way you walked out with such great determination last night." Her grin broadened. "It wasn't the rejection that bothered me so much, but the circumstances. When a girl is rejected while stark naked, it does shake her self-confidence! It makes you start wondering; if that's not enough, then just what else have you got to offer?"

"You fouled it up in the beginning," I said seriously. "The way you talked, it sounded like you wanted us to set up a mutual comfort station for the night. Romantic, it wasn't!"

"I'll have to remember that the next time, Rick." Her smile slowly faded. "You didn't visit just to advise me on the gentle art of seducing the male?"

"I figured it was my last chance to separate the lies from the truth," I brushed past her and plunked myself down on the couch. "There's no need to rush it, I've got all night."

"You're impossible," she groaned, then sat down on the couch as far away from me as she could.

I told her Jackie Slater's story of how Hugill had called her from his office at Wallace Productions, dangled a part in their new movie in front of her, then dined and bedded her. How he had been fascinated in the details of her married life with Sam Sorel, right up until the time she told him about Sorel's sudden attack on her a couple of days after it had happened. How she never saw him again after that, and the final brush-off had been brutally effective.

"So?" Her voice was carefully devoid of expression.

"He made a play for Linda Galen, too, but he couldn't get past the guardian dragon, Andrea Marco, and he finally gave up trying," I said. "I guess it was a little too tough for even a guy like Hugill to come between their peculiar relationship."

"There's a kind of macabre fascination in your sordid anecdotes, Rick." She covered her yawn after she'd made sure I'd seen it. "But why bother telling me?"

"Some guy called Shelley offered you—right out of left field—the chance of a job with Reynor Plastics. He even invited you to a party, where you met Hugill. After that, Shelly and the job both faded quietly out of the picture. Did you know Hugill is a silent partner in Reynor Plastics?"

"Who told you that?"

"Sonia Mayer."

Her face froze. "It so happens I didn't know Roger had an interest in the company. Is there more?"

"Loads!" I grinned nastily at her. "Somebody—I'm not sure who at the moment—asked for a confidential report on Sam's three ex-wives a few months back. My guess is they got one copy, and Hugill the other. He's also a silent partner in Trushman, of course, and that information comes from the same source, Sonia Mayer. There's lovable Roger with the lowdown on the activities, both public and intimate, of Sam Sorel's ex-wives. He goes to a hell of a lot of trouble to arrange a meeting with them, then build the relationships to the point where they sleep with him—and scores two out of three." I paused a moment to give it an extra thrust. "Two out of three, Beverly. You and Jackie Slater. What kind of a man does that make Rober Hugill, I wonder?"

She sat there with two bright-red spots burning on her cheeks, vivid enough to match the color of her hair, and I could see the deep hurt in her eyes.

"If he ever mentioned marriage to you, which I doubt," I said cruelly, "he was talking about the moon. The only kind of wife that creep is interested in either belongs, or belonged, to some other guy. I figure he gets his kicks that way, and maybe it's the only way he can get his kicks."

"I need a drink," she whispered.

"I need the truth. Maybe we can trade?"

I got up from the couch, made a couple of drinks at the bar and brought them back. She took the glass from my hand and drank about half its contents. Then she looked up at me and I saw that the hurt in her eyes had been replaced by a cold fury.

"I've got my drink, so now it's your turn to collect on the trade," she said in a brittle voice.

"The first time I walked in here you knew all about me because Sam called around six thirty last night, loaded, and told you I was coming. True?"

"A lie," she said flatly. "It was Roger who called and told me about you. He also said to tell you that story about Sam busting in here a couple of weeks back and threatening to beat me up. When I asked why, he said he didn't have the time to explain fully right then, but if I didn't it would make me the number one suspect as Sam's potential murderer."

"Sam figures you never called him in the first place and it was someone impersonating your voice."

"I never called him."

"You did what Hugill asked, you lied to me about Sam's visit and his call. Then you steered me onto Hugill." I looked at her curiously. "I don't get it."

Her eyes met mine and she tried to smile. "A woman is a complex thing, Rick! Roger gave me the brush-off about a month back. When he suddenly called last night, I was flattered at first, then I got mad at him when I realized he was just using me. So I thought I'd get back at him through you. And you're right, incidentally, at no time during our brief intimate relationship did he ever even mention the word marriage!"

"Why did you keep on pushing the nympho bit at me?"

"It made for a better story." She grimaced sharply.

"No, that isn't true. Inside my crazy, mixed-up mind I guess I figured if you did see Roger—you'd mention it to him. I had a very faint hope that it might make him feel jealous."

"The second time I was here last night, you looked like you were dressed to entertain a visitor. Certainly, you weren't expecting me."

"I told you a half-truth when I said Roger called me. He called to say he was coming straight over here. I wanted to look my best for him. When he came he told me about Linda Galen having been murdered, and he also mentioned that Sam and the Mayer woman were coming to stay at his house for the next two weeks. He was furious because I'd given you his name." She shivered slightly. "I'd never seen him like that before. An ice-cold, implacable determination to get his own way. He said if I didn't stick by the story I'd told you earlier about Sam—both to you and the police—he'd arrange for me to have an accident. Nothing fatal; a mugging and a rape, possibly. He was very graphic about the details. After a multiple rape, a beating bad enough to hospitalize me for a few weeks. He couldn't make a guess about how long the mental scars would last, he said. They would probably be a psychiatrist's problem." She swallowed some more of her drink. "What really scared the hell out of me was the way he said it, Rick, in that cold, unemotional voice. I know instinctively that it was the kind of thing he could—and would—arrange, without even thinking twice about it."

"Is that why you offered me your all last night?"

She nodded. "I was so frightened you might go back to Roger again after you left here, and he'd think it was my fault." She managed a smile this time. "I'm sorry I forgot to make it sound more enticing, but I wasn't exactly in a romantic frame of mind at the time."

"Sure," I grinned back at her. "Did the lieutenant see you today?"

"Around six tonight."

"You stayed with the same stories about Sam that Hugill told you to repeat?"

"Yes. Lieutenant Santana didn't seem that interested. He just kept nodding the whole time."

"You were just substantiating his theory that the obvious suspect is the guilty party at the time," I told her. "He's got Sam fingered at the scene of the crime, at the right time, and with a strong motive. Your story strengthened his case by adding to Sam's apparently wide background of violence. You didn't mention Hugill to him?"

"I didn't think this was my day for a multiple rape and hospitalization," she said in a low voice.

"Maybe you'll need to take Sam off the hook with the lieutenant—at least as far as your story is concerned—sometime tomorrow," I said. "But we'll wait and see if I can fix Hugill's bandwagon first."

"You can't stop a man like Roger," she said flatly. "He's too strong, too ruthless, and he's got too much power! You'd be crazy to try, Rick."

"Maybe I can make a trade with him?"

"Like what?"

"I'm not sure." I shrugged. "I guess all those bird pictures have to be worth something?"

She laughed softly. "I'd forgotten about those monstrosities!"

I finished my drink and stood up. "I'll let you know how the trade works out."

"Now I'm scared more than ever, for the both of us." She got onto her feet and stood facing me for a moment, her eyes glowing with a sudden warmth. "You're a crazy guy, Rick Holman! A paranoiac, with delusions of grandeur, I shouldn't be surprised!"

Then she suddenly threw her arms around my neck and kissed me fiercely on the lips. I was caught off-balance so it took me a whole half second to respond. We stayed locked in a tight clinch for what seemed a long time, until she finally broke away.

"That was no kind of an offer," she said shakily. "Just an expression of feeling, you understand?"

"I understand," I nodded. "But even just an expression of feeling means something more when it comes from a genuine redhead like you."

She almost blushed. "Why don't you get the hell out of here?"

"You've been saying that ever since I arrived," I

said plaintively. "I always try to be cooperative, so I'll leave now."

My appointment with Hugill was for eleven, and it was only ten after nine when I got back to the car. I was going to be early, but I felt reasonably sure he'd listen to what I had to say, even if I had to wave a gun at him to get inside the house. My mind went back to its favorite topic—women—during the drive to Brentwood. Beverly was still real fresh in my memory. Then I thought about the pneumatic starlet, Jackie Slater, using my house as a hideout to escape being murdered. The connotations of that word reminded me of Linda Galen. Sam Sorel must have a hell of a lot of hidden talent, I figured, to have married three very different women like that. Linda—the attractive, womanly brunet; Beverly—the intelligent and vital redhead; Jackie—the dumb, silver-blonde starlet with all those fantastic curves. And don't forget the fourth, my memory said sourly. Sure, he hasn't married her as yet but you can make book that she's been more than a wife to him over the last couple of years. Sonia Mayer—the cool blonde, the one that made me flip the first time I saw her. The girl who was so crazy about Sorel she was even ready to force herself to sleep with me if it would help him in any way at all.

So why not become a claustrophobic comic, Holman? I asked myself. Then you, too, can be a big success with women. There was only one answer to that—I didn't know any funny jokes. There are times when even *I* wonder if I'm sane.

I parked the car out front of the house, walked up the driveway to the front porch, and rang the doorbell. It took two seconds, at most, for the door to open. A guy I had never seen before stood there, watching me very carefully. He was around thirty, average height, and a little on the lean side. His brown hair had a neat, orthodox part in it, and his face was kind of nondescript. But he had a couple of features I found real impressive. The cold, dark eyes that watched me so intently from under hooded lids, and the way he kept his right hand tucked inside his coat the whole time.

"You want something?" His voice was soft and slightly sibilant.

"To see Mr. Hugill," I told him. "My name's Holman."

"If you're Holman, you're early," he said. "Holman's appointment is for eleven tonight. So if you're Holman, come back then. If you're not Holman, come back anytime and I'll beat your skull in, just for laughs!"

"What is it, Eddie?" A self-possessed contralto voice asked from someplace in back of him.

"No trouble, Miss Mayer," he said, without taking his eyes off me for a moment. "A guy called, Holman—he says—but he's not expected before eleven."

Sonia's face showed up behind his left shoulder. "It's all right," she said. "This is Mr. Holman and I wish to talk with him."

Eddie's lips tightened into a thin line of disapproval, then he shrugged imperceptibly and moved to one side. I took a step past him, then froze as I felt a gun barrel dig hard into the small of my back. His free hand expertly frisked me and lifted the thirty-eight from the belt holster.

"You get it back when you leave, friend," he hissed. "Mr. Hugill wouldn't like for me to let you into his house carrying hardware."

There was nothing I could do about it, so I followed Sonia into the cluttered living room. She closed the door carefully when we got inside, then smiled.

"Eddie isn't exactly the trusting type!"

"Whose idea is Eddie?" I growled.

"Roger's. He said maybe you were busy finding out who killed Linda Galen, which was dandy, but meanwhile—back at the Hugill ranch—who was to stop anybody from carrying out those murder threats against Sam?"

I was busy getting that breathless feeling just looking at her. She was wearing a black sleeveless dress with a wicked V-neckline that plunged almost to the depths of her cleavage. The glittering horizontal silver streak around her hips was a sparkling contrast to the rest of the basic black. The tiny copper bell still dangled from her bite-sized earlobe, and I wondered wistfully if it would ever tinkle just for me?

"Rick?" Her gray-green eyes were laughing at me. "Did you hear what I just said?"

"Sure," I mumbled, then had to clear my throat. "Eddie was Hugill's idea."

She smiled. "Well, you can't be everywhere at the same time, Rick."

"Leave us hope the same applies to Eddie," I said. "Where's Sam?"

"In his room watching television. They're running a repeat of a Terry Crane special he made last year. Sam did a five-minute bit toward the end, and he's like the rest of showbiz people—he can't wait to see himself again."

"Hugill?"

"Roger went out a while back, I don't know where. He said he wouldn't be long. Can I fix you a drink, Rick?"

"Bourbon on the rocks, thanks."

She threaded her way around the confusion of furniture that littered the room until she reached the bar at the far end. I looked at the painting on the wall nearest to me, and figured the artist must have been insane at the time. Either that, or how come I had never heard of the double-headed fantailed shrike before?

I wondered how a man with Hugill's money could have such ridiculous ideas about spending it. The way the room was decorated wouldn't have done credit to anyone, and the furniture wasn't only ghastly looking, it wasn't even expensive! Even rich people with poor taste don't go around buying cheap junk. Not if they care the least bit about their image.

So maybe Hugill didn't care. So maybe he didn't have to care.

"Come and sit down over here, Rick," Sonia called. "There's a couch that's almost comfortable."

By the time I got there she was already sitting at one end of the couch. I looked doubtfully at the four spindly legs supporting the front of it and she gurgled with laughter.

I sat down cautiously and she handed me the drink.

"You've known Hugill a long time," I said. "I guess you consider him a good friend?"

"A very good friend," she nodded.

"A guy you can trust to help out when you're in trouble?"

"Yes, I think so," she answered in a relaxed voice.

"A guy like him, a silent partner in about anything you care to name, would be a definite asset," I agreed. "You want to get into movies—he's right there at Wallace Productions; you've got a plastics problem—he's right there at Reynor Plastics; you want the lowdown on the private lives of Sam Sorel's three ex-wives—he's right there at the Trushman Detective Agency!"

Sonia sat very still. I drank some bourbon while I watched her face jell into an expressionless mold.

"Maybe you had a good reason?" I said, after a while.

"Sam had just about hit bottom when he asked me to become his personal manager. He was a little psychotic then, and there were many times during the long haul back up the ladder when we had nothing else to do but sit around and talk." A reminiscent smile hovered on her lips. "It was more like I listened while he talked. I heard all the stories of his three marriages over and over a thousand times, and I didn't mind because it was a kind of emotional therapy for him. But it got so those three women became very real to me. I knew so much about them; the way they looked, dressed, talked, and almost the way they thought. The time for me to worry about them was when Sam was back on top again. He's still a child, emotionally, and if they started getting at him I knew he'd fall apart at the seams."

She shook her head slowly and the little copper bell tolled for the hopes of Holman, I figured. "The way I saw it, we needed a card up our sleeve to keep them where they belonged, out of Sam's life. I knew Roger had an interest in the detective agency, so I asked him to get a confidential report on the three women, especially their private lives. The idea was to give it to Sam, then if any one of them started pestering him, he'd know the truth. Only when I saw the report I knew Sam wouldn't believe it, because he wouldn't want to believe it. But somehow, for his own sake, he had to know."

"It was you that called him and faked their voices over the phone?"

She nodded. "It wasn't hard. He hadn't spoken with any of them in years, and if a voice sounded strange to him it could be just a bad connection. I'm not especially proud of it, Rick; it was just something that had to be done for his own sake."

"If you'd left well enough alone, he wouldn't have gotten involved with Linda again, and maybe she'd still be alive right now."

"That thought has also occurred to me," she said stiffly.

"There's more," I said, then told her about Hugill using the report as the basis for a seduction campaign that resulted in a score of two out of three. I gave her chapter and verse, leaving nothing out, including his threats to Beverly Quillen if she didn't go along with him. Sonia looked like she'd been hit with a baseball bat by the time I had finished.

"I know it has to be true," she said in a soft contralto that didn't sound self-possessed anymore. "It's just that it's going to take a little while before I can accept it."

The door opened and Sam Sorel came into the room. He was wearing that faded robe over a pair of pajamas, and his face looked haggard. "Sonia?" His wandering gaze finally hit the couch. "There you are!" He started toward us slowly. "Hi, Rick. When are you going to take that goddamned lieutenant off my back?"

"Real soon, I think," I told him.

"We had another session this afternoon." He stopped in front of the couch and ran his fingers quickly through his long, graying hair. "The same goddamned questions over and over until I could have screamed in his face!"

"How was the Terry Crane repeat?" Sonia asked.

"Lousy." He grinned momentarily. "But I was great!" He let out a cavernous yawn. "Brother, I'm beat! You know where that Nembutal is, honey?"

"In the small attaché case on top of your bureau," she answered promptly. "But don't start eating them like candy. Two are plenty."

"Sure, sure!" He nodded. "You get that lieutenant off my back, Rick, and then I'll start to relax. With you and Eddie around to keep tabs on the house, I'll stop worrying about being murdered in my bed."

"Sure thing, Sam," I said. "Tell me something. You married three women who all had a hell of a lot going for them, and now you've got Sonia, who maybe has even more going for her than the other three combined. You're not young anymore, Sam. You're ugly and neurotic, and I'd figure you have less sex appeal than a giraffe. So how the hell do you do it?"

The wrinkled skin tightened over his face as his jaw locked. I looked into the mournful dark-brown eyes and saw the naked despair that he couldn't hide mirrored there.

"You stinking son of a bitch!" He nearly choked on the words. "I hope you wind up in a sewer someplace, where you belong!" Then he turned away quickly and stumbled out of the room, knocking a couple of chairs out of his way with a blind indifference.

"So what did I say?" I asked, appealing to Sonia, the moment after the door slammed shut in back of him.

"It wasn't your fault, Rick." The tone of her voice said different. "It was, well, unfortunate. I think I should go up and stay with him for a while, until he goes to sleep, anyway."

I watched the firm bounce of her silver-streaked bottom as she walked across the room and couldn't help wondering if she was about to play Mother Earth again. The door closed behind her and I waited a couple of minutes before I went over to the phone. Marco was listed in the book, so I dialed the number. Andrea answered, her voice dull.

"This is Rick Holman," I said. "I want you and your brother to come over to Brentwood. Get here before eleven."

"What for?"

"I figure the both of you are entitled to know who killed Linda Galen."

107

"I know who killed her!" Her voice became ugly. "That bastard, Sorel!"

"Maybe," I said, "maybe not. If you want to know for sure, be here before eleven."

"All right," she snapped. "What's the address?"

I gave it to her, then hung up. As I headed toward the bar to get another drink the walls all around me seemed full of birds of prey, waiting expectantly.

CHAPTER TEN

Maybe a half hour later Hugill came striding confidently into the room with a satisfied sneer visible under his bristling moustache. He made a big deal out of checking his watch the moment before he reached the bar.

"You're still thirty minutes early for your appointment, Holman," he barked. "But it's not important; this won't take very long at all. It's only a matter of simple choice."

"How did you manage to get to Harv Graham, the manager of the motor court?" I asked idly.

It threw him for a second, then he shrugged. "I called him and told him if he or Jackie talked to you about me, I'd not only see he was fired from the motor court, but I'd also make goddamned sure he was blacklisted throughout the whole industry." His gray eyes were watchful. "I thought he was impressed."

"He was," I agreed. "But when I told Jackie it was you who killed Linda Galen, and she was the next victim on your list, she stopped being impressed and started getting nervous."

He laughed shortly. "I'll admit you do have a certain flare at times, Holman. However" -his face hardened again—"I think we should get down to the basic discussion."

"Like what do you want from me to stop you from turning in that Trushman operative's report to the police?"

"Precisely!"

He started in leisurely making himself a drink. I lit a cigarette to cover the gap where, presumably, I was meant to start sweating with anxiety. It was an interesting conjecture, wondering if his mother had been a monster or had just reared one.

"Eddie!" he called sharply. I studied him evenly, wondering if he was enjoying playing his game of nerves. One thing for sure, it took a lot of nerve to be so obvious about it!

The thin man with the gun appeared at the door as if by magic. He nodded at his boss and glanced eagerly at me.

"Find Sonia, Eddie," Hugill smiled pleasantly. "Just watch her. Mr. Holman and I wouldn't like to be unexpectedly interrupted. Would we Rick?"

"Speak for yourself," I grated. "Now what's the price? And remember, I'm not as rich as you, so I don't have as much to lose."

Eddie disappeared without a sound, while Hugill finished his drink.

"I want you to help the police convict the Galen woman's murderer," he said finally.

"Who is?" I queried.

"Sorel, who else? It's quite simple, Holman. All you need to do is make a statement saying you were going to see her last night, following up the threatening letters Sorel had received. Then, just as you parked your car close to the apartment building, you saw Sorel sneak out of the service area, run to his car, and drive away."

"Santana is going to ask one real awkward question," I said. "Like, why didn't I tell him this last night?"

"There's a very simple answer," he barked. "You had a conflict of loyalties because Sorel was your client. It took some time wrestling with your conscience, but you finally decided you had to be an upright, virtuous citizen. He may even give you a medal."

"I guess you never will get close to Sonia while Sam is still around," I said conversationally.

His face darkened. "We'll leave Sonia out of this. I'm waiting for your answer, Holman."

"I know about the confidential report you got through the Trushman Agency for Sonia," I told him. "And how you contrived to meet Jackie Slater and Beverly Quillen—and finally seduced them. You didn't make out so well with Linda Galen because she had a special relationship with Andrea Marco. Maybe you can't take failure. So maybe you killed her out of frustration."

"That's too goddamned stupid to argue about!" he snapped.

"You're about the worst kind of womanizer, Hugill," I sneered. "The kind that always has to have some other guy's woman, or women. I'll make a deal with you; put a match to that Trushman operative's report about me and I'll keep my mouth shut about your private life."

"You've got to be kidding!"

"Okay," I shrugged easily, "so I'll spread the word about you, and how you went chasing Sorel's ex-wives. You know the kind of contacts I've got around this town. Who knows? By the time they've finished laughing they could even make you an offer for the film rights. The story could make a smash-hit low comedy!"

The rich color on his face ripened into a full flush as he stared at me. A brisk knock on the door broke the tension for a moment as we both turned our heads to see the bodyguard walk into the room.

"What is it?" Hugill rasped.

"I left a guy and a dame the wrong side of the front door," Eddie said. "Name of Marco. They say Holman called them and said to come over here?"

"Is that right?" Hugill glowered at me.

"Sure," I nodded. "I figured they had a right to be here when I prove just who did kill Linda Galen."

"You still think it was me?"

I grinned at him nastily. "You scared to find out?"

He swallowed a quick mouthful of his drink, then put the glass back down on the bar, his jaw rigid. "Show them in, Eddie."

"Sure, Mr. Hugill."

"And, Eddie, stay just the other side of the door afterward. I could need you in here fast."

"Okay, Mr. Hugill. But what about Miss Mayer?"

"Forget her!" Hugill snapped. "Do like I said."

The bodyguard gave me a vague smile before he left the room, and it didn't do that empty feeling inside my belt holster any good at all.

I looked at Hugill again. "I guess our deal is going to have to wait for a while?"

"Maybe forever." His voice was thoughtful. "I usually make sure people are in no position to argue about anything I want done, and I'm beginning to realize I'd be a fool to make an exception in your case."

The door opened again and Andrea Marco walked into the room, followed by her brother. Her long blond hair swung gently below her shoulders, and her eyes were hidden behind large dark glasses. She was wearing a back crepe mini-shift which didn't quite reach halfway down her thighs, black lace stockings, and black low-heeled shoes with large silver buckles. The overall effect was bizarre, but also sexy in a macabre kind of way. Frank was wearing a shabby sportcoat, turtlenecked sweater, and a pair of creased pants that looked like he had been sleeping in them for the last week. They stood awkwardly for a moment as Eddie gently closed himself out of the room.

"This is Andrea Marco and her brother, Frank," I told Hugill.

"He's the one that pestered Linda in the boutique for a while," Andrea said in a flat voice. "I recognize him now."

"He's the one who got a copy of the confidential report on Sorel's three ex-wives and their intimate lives," I told her. "Sonia Mayer asked him to get it because she was scared that one or more of them might put the bite on Sam now that he was getting back on top. But Mr. Hugill used his copy as a blueprint for seduction; he's a little kinky about other guy's wives, and even their ex-wives."

"I don't care about that," she said abruptly. "We only came here because you said you could prove who killed Linda. I *know* Sorel killed her, and I'd like to see you prove any different!"

"I have to do it my way," I rasped. "When Sonia Mayer got the report she knew it would be a waste of time showing it to Sam—he just wouldn't believe it—so she made those phone calls, pretending each time to be one of his ex-wives. That's why Sam came busting into Linda's apartment a few months back."

She yawned. "You're boring me, Holman."

"Sis," Frank's high-pitched voice was conciliatory, "I think it's only right we should hear Mr. Holman out."

"The real tragedy of Linda's death," I said soberly, "is that it was caused by a whole chain of good intentions."

"Just what the hell is that supposed to mean?" Andrea snarled.

"Sonia Mayer got the report and made the phone calls to protect Sam, as she thought, from the predatory instincts of his ex-wives. If she hadn't done that, the chances are Sam would never have met Linda again, and they wouldn't have fallen in love for a second time."

"That's a filthy lie!" Her mouth set in a firm line.

"Frank?" I appealed to him. "You know it's the truth, right?"

The haunted look showed up in his watery blue eyes while he fingered his swollen lip nervously. "Well"—his voice cracked suddenly—"I'm not too sure, exactly, Mr. Holman."

"You were sure enough around noon today." I shrugged. "Anyway, Santana checked it out and it's a matter of record; times and places." It was a reasonable lie, I figured, because nobody was about to call the lieutenant and ask him. "So then"—I looked at Andrea again—"you had your big problem. How to stop Linda from leaving you and going back to Sam. You moved her into your own apartment on the excuse she'd be better protected there from him, what with your brother living right across the hall. But what you really wanted was for Frank to keep an eye on her when you couldn't. Then, with the best of intentions, you set out to bust the rapidly developing relationship between the two of them."

"And just how, exactly, did I do that?" she asked.

"You started sending Sam those letters," I said. "The murder threats that apparently had to come from one of his ex-wives, and he'd have to consider Linda as a possibility. My guess is you intended to keep working on it until he had no choice but believe it was Linda, only she was murdered before you had the chance."

She pulled off the dark glasses and her blue eyes were baleful. "If you're trying to say I killed Linda, you're out of your mind! Lieutenant Santana checked out that fashion preview. A dozen people told him I was there—never even left the room—between eight and ten-fifteen that night!"

"I was just talking about good intentions," I said easily. "Your letters made Sam so nervous he called me in. Sonia Mayer didn't want that, but there was nothing she could do about it. She warned our friend Mr. Hugill here about me; the last thing she wanted was for me to find out about the report and tell Sam. My talking with Linda and you in the boutique that morning stepped up the pressure on the both of you. Up until that time Linda had been scared to make the final break with you and go back to Sam. But early that night she decided she would; she called Sam, then she called me. I figure she had guessed by then who was writing those murder threats and she intended to tell me."

"Crazy talk!" she whispered.

"The last thing you wanted was to go to that fashion preview, but you couldn't get out of it," I said. "So you warned Frank to keep a close watch on your apartment in case Sam showed up."

"Holman!" Hugill said in a thin voice. "I think we've listened to you running off at the mouth long enough. Let me ask you one question: who the hell did kill the Galen woman?"

"The invisible man," I told him. "The guy who was there the whole time and nobody ever gave him a second thought afterward."

He closed his eyes for a moment. "You mean, Sorel?"

I looked across at Andrea and held her gaze. "In the club manager's office last night everybody, including the lieutenant, was convinced Sam was lying. But everything he said then was checked out as true. Somebody—Sonia Mayer—did fake those voices over the phone. He had fallen in love with Linda again and she was about to come back to him. He didn't go see Beverly Quillen; she lied about that because Mr. Hugill here told her to and she was scared of crossing him. The one person who comes off like George Washington in all this is Sam Sorel."

"You're still trying to protect your client," she sneered.

"Frank stopped him from going inside the apartment and he left, remember?" I said.

"Oh, sure! Then he went around the back and came in through the service area!"

"Sam said it out loud last night, but nobody was listening to him. Frank stopped him in the hallway and said he wasn't getting into your apartment. Then, and I quote, Sam said they argued for a couple of minutes until he pulled a knife on him and he got scared he'd use it, so he left."

"Are you trying to say that Frank killed Linda?" She laughed hysterically. "That's the funniest thing I ever heard!"

"The invisible man," I said coldly. "Standing there with a knife in his hand, but nobody even listened to Sorel tell it because they were already sure he was the murderer."

"Mr. Holman." Frank's face twitched suddenly. "Why would I want to kill Linda?"

"Out of desperation, I guess." At that moment I almost felt sorry for him. "Things weren't exactly the same between you and your sister after Linda came into Andrea's life. I guess you hoped she'd just vanish one day so things could get back to what they had been before. Then Sam Sorel showed up, and Andrea kept telling you she was relying on you to make sure Linda didn't get together with Sorel while she wasn't around to prevent it. Maybe when he showed up last night it was your breaking-point. You stopped him then, but could you stop him again? You knew your sister had already written those murder threats, and maybe if the situation got any worse she'd carry them out."

I smiled at him, then talked in a quiet sympathetic voice. "It wasn't really fair to you, Frank, was it? Something had to be done to stop it from developing into an unbearable situation for you. Either Linda would slip away with Sorel one of those times without you being able to stop her or, worse, Andrea would be driven to carrying out her threats, and murder Sorel. Whichever way it happened, you would have lost your sister forever, and whose fault was it?"

"It was all her fault!" The tears started slowly trickling down his pudgy cheeks. "I can't tell you the agonies I suffered because of that bitch! It all came to me in the hallway last night after Sorel had gone. There was only one answer, Mr. Holman. I had to kill Linda to save Andrea!" His whole body started quivering gently. "I'm so glad you understand, Mr. Holman. It's been haunting me ever since." He pressed the back of his hand tight against his mouth for a long moment. "The dreadful thing was that once I started, I couldn't stop! I knew she must have been dead after the second time I stabbed her, but I hated her so much for what she'd done to Andrea and me, I just kept on and on"—his voice broke into a harsh sob—"and on!"

Andrea hit him across the mouth with the back of her hand and kept on hitting him until he went down on his knees and tried to clasp her legs. She responded by kicking him viciously in the stomach and sent him sprawling onto the floor. He lay there sobbing for a few seconds, then slowly curled himself into a football at her feet. She looked up and I felt a sudden shock as I realized the glittering hatred in her eyes was not for her brother but for me.

"It's still Sorel's fault," she snarled. "If he hadn't tried to take Linda away from me, it would never have happened!"

"I agree entirely," Hugill said in a self-righteous voice.

"You—what?" I gaped at him.

"Sorel is morally responsible for everything, and he's the one who should pay the penalty." He kept his eyes fixed on Andrea as he spoke. "I don't see what's just happened here makes any difference at all. I feel sure we can persuade your brother he was only suffering from an overwrought imagination, Miss Marco."

A faint gleam of hope came into her eyes, then died. "I'm sure we could, Mr. Hugill, but I doubt if we could persuade Holman."

"I think you can safely leave that problem to me," he said briskly.

"You want Sonia that bad?" I asked him. "You'd let Sorel go to the gas chamber for a murder you know he didn't commit, just to get him out of the way?"

"I've never let anything—or anyone—stand in the way of something I want," he barked, "that goes for Sorel, and you, Holman!"

Frank slowly uncurled his body and came up onto her knees. His long blond hair had fallen down over his forehead, and there was a kind of boyish adoration in his eyes as he lifted his tear-stained face and looked up at Andrea.

His sister stared down at him coldly and kicked him hard in the right kidney. "All right, loving brother," she sneered, "get up. You're not dead yet."

"There is one thing before we go any further," Hugill said, and I saw the flush creeping up his neck as he stared deliberately at Andrea. "If I'm going to take the risks involved in saving your brother from the gas chamber, Miss Marco, I shall certainly expect something from you in return."

"Like what?" she asked.

"Well!" He shrugged meaningfully. "Your appreciation, affectionately expressed, of course!"

Her mouth twisted savagely. "If it's all right with my brother," she said with bitter sarcasm.

Frank made a small whimpering sound deep in his throat, squeezed his eyes shut tight, then nodded quickly.

"Brother approves!" Andrea grimaced. "That leaves one problem—Holman."

Hugill turned his head toward me and smiled happily. "I don't think he's about to present any great problem, Miss Marco. Eddie relieved him of his gun when he came into the house. Eddie is very efficient. I'm sure he'll be delighted to arrange something fatal for Holman, like an auto accident."

"You know something?" I grated. "I figure you're not only a paranoiac, but a paranoiac with delusions of paranoia!"

"After you're dead," he said in a casual voice, "I shall give the Trushman operative's report to the police. That will place both you and Sorel at the scene of the murder, and at the right time. I don't know what they'll make of it, of course. Some form of collusion, maybe? And if your fatal auto accident looks like it could have been suicide?" He shrugged expressively. "Well, in any case, I don't imagine it will help Sorel any when he stands trial!"

The bodyguard, I remembered while Hugill was still listening to the sound of his own voice, was right outside the door. From the way he looked at me, I figured he could be a little trigger-happy. I mentally crossed my fingers that he was a hell of a lot more than just a little that way.

"You're overlooking one factor, Hugill," I said in a tense voice. "It won't work. You'll never get away with it. You want to know why?"

"Tell me." He grinned affably. "I don't believe you, but I'm always open to suggestion."

"Him!" I said, and pointed toward Frank Marco.

"What about him?" Hugill sneered, his eyes automatically following the direction of my pointing finger.

I swung around and hit Hugill in the solar plexus with all the power I could get behind my clenched fist. His eyes rolled as the air exploded out of his lungs, and his body started to sag forward. From behind him I wrapped one arm around his neck real tight to keep him upright and stop him from yelling. Then I grabbed his left wrist with my free hand and wound his arm up tight behind his back. The next moment I started propelling him toward the door, gathering momentum with each successive step.

"Okay, Hugill!" I yelled at the top of my lungs when we were about ten feet from the door. "You asked for that knife in your ribs! I'm getting out of here right now, and if anybody tries to stop me I'll use the goddamn knife again!"

The moment I saw the door open I let go my hold on Hugill's neck and used both hands to launch him toward it. There was the explosive staccato sound of two quick shots in succession. His body seemed to stop momentarily in midair, then fell in a heap on the floor. Eddie stood framed in the doorway, holding the gun in his right hand, a dazed expression on his face.

"Shoot me," I said quickly, "and there goes your only witness that it was an accident!"

"I figured it was you!" His voice shook a little. "I could have sworn I heard you yelling something about you'd knifed Mr. Hugill and—"

"You must have been confused!" a high-pitched voice said beside me.

Frank Marco walked past me toward the bodyguard, a fixed smile on his face. "It was Mr. Hugill that shouted out. He lost his temper over something. But don't worry, Eddie. We can all testify it was an unfortunate accident. Please give me the gun now."

"Sure," Eddie muttered, and handed him the gun.

"Hey!" I yelled, but it had been handled too smoothly and too fast.

"Thank you!" Frank smiled gratefully as he took the gun.

The next moment he thrust the barrel up against the roof of his mouth and pulled the trigger.

CHAPTER ELEVEN

Andrea Marco gave a thin scream the moment after her brother killed himself, then fainted. The long blond hair fell across her face and the black crepe mini-shift was hiked up around the tops of her thighs, revealing the full length of her long slender legs, which looked both elegant yet somehow pathetic.

Eddie looked like he was about to follow her onto the floor. His face was a nasty gray color, and his forehead was covered with sweat.

"What the hell goes on around here?" he muttered, then grabbed hold of the nearest chair for support.

"It's a good question," I told him. "The trouble is, it needs one hell of a long answer."

A loud groan made Eddie nearly hit the ceiling. I walked over to where Hugill lay face down on the floor, went down on my knees, and gently rolled him over onto his back.

"I'm dying!" His eyes stared up at me wildly, filled with terror. "Get me a doctor, Holman. For God's sake!"

"If I were you, after that auto accident you were going to arrange for me," I grunted, "you'd get me a doctor, right?" He nodded eagerly. "The hell you would!" I snarled. "You'd back up and run the rear wheels over me again!"

"Please!" he whimpered. "Maybe there's still a chance!"

There was plenty of blood, and I was vaguely surprised to see it was the usual color and not the bright yellow I had expected. One slug had taken him high in the right shoulder and the other had gone straight through his right forearm. The only thing likely to kill him right then was his own panic.

"You'll live," I told him, "provided you get a doctor soon. So now is the time to make that deal."

"Deal?" His eyes nearly popped out of his head. "Are you insane? Call that goddamned doctor!"

"No deal, no doctor, Mr. Hugill." I grinned coldly at him. "I should worry if you bleed to death?"

"All right!" His mouth writhed under the moustache that had wilted. "What deal?"

"I was never here," I said. "The way you tell it to Santana is that after talking to Sam Sorel you began to suspect that Marco could be the real killer. You invited both of them to your house, under the pretext you'd found out something that would help incriminate Sam. You had Eddie, the bodyguard you hired to protect Sam, stay close in case of trouble. After a while you got Andrea to admit her brother had been in love with Linda, and that's why she'd tried to shield him by pretending she had a relationship with her. Then he got into a hysterical fury and started screaming at the both of you and admitted he sent the threatening letters to Sam. When they didn't work he decided he'd prefer to have Linda dead than see her go back to Sam, so he killed her. You got that?"

"Yes!" Hugill grated. "Make it fast, will you? I'm losing blood all the time you're talking!"

"You've got pints left yet," I growled. "He suddenly came at you in a kind of manic frenzy—you yelled out for Eddie—then Marco grabbed you, spun you around, and forced you toward the door, yelling at the top of his voice he'd kill anybody who got in his way. Eddie opened the door, saw somebody hurtling toward him and figured it was Marco, so he started shooting. He was so shocked when he realized it was you he'd shot, he dropped the gun. Marco grabbed it and killed himself. Okay?"

"How about the sister?" he muttered. "She'll never go along with that!"

"Sure she will," I said confidently. "The only alternative is the truth. You figure she would ever want to admit the real reason why her brother killed Linda Galen?"

"I guess you're right."

"I'm being generous," I told him. "You'll come out of this smelling of roses. Maybe the lieutenant will give you a medal."

He closed his eyes tight. "Now will you call that goddamned doctor!"

I got back onto my feet, then walked over to where Eddie was still holding tight to the chair. "You heard that?" I asked him.

"Yeah," he nodded quickly. "It was an accident. The creep yells out he's going to kill anybody who gets in his way. I figure maybe he's killed the boss already. I open the door and this guy comes straight at me, so I let him have it. I'm so shocked to find out it's the boss who collected the slugs that I drop the gun, and the creep—"

"You've got it!" I said quickly. "Call a doctor for Mr. Hugill. He's not hurt bad at all, and there's no chance of him dying no matter what he tells you."

"That's good!" His face brightened a little and he let go of the chair.

"Give it ten minutes after you've called the doctor, then call Lieutenant Santana of the homicide bureau. Tell him your hero-type boss has just solved the Galen murder and risked death in the process."

"Ten minutes after I've called the doc," he nodded.

"And give me back my gun!"

"It's in the front hall on the bureau." He grinned faintly. "Those magnums always make me feel nervous. Lucky I didn't use it on the boss, huh?"

I collected the thirty-eight from the bureau, then went upstairs. The light was on in the main bedroom and the door was wide open, so I walked straight in without knocking. Sonia Mayer was sitting at the head of the bed, her dress peeled down to her waist, her arms around Sorel's shoulders, cradling his head against her bare breasts. She looked up as I came into the room and smiled uncertainly.

"The sound of the shots disturbed him," she said

softly. "He started having one of his nightmares again, but I think he's all right now."

"He didn't even wake up?"

"Nembutal! By the time I'd gotten up here he'd taken more than those two tablets I said were his limit."

"The shots didn't worry you any?" I asked wonderingly.

"They worried me all right, but there was nothing I could do about whatever had happened downstairs."

"You didn't even want to go and find out what had happened?"

"Sam needed me here. What did happen, Rick?"

I told her the story, keeping it as brief as possible. Her face relaxed by the time I finished, and she smiled radiantly.

"That means Sam is safe, and he doesn't have to worry anymore!" Her voice caught for a moment. "We're beholden to you, Rick!"

"That's easily fixed, I'll bill you!" I grinned, then felt my face stiffen. "Sam is a very lucky guy."

"You think so?" There was a sudden hard edge to her contralto voice. "I think he's the unluckiest guy in the whole world, Rick."

"He's got you." I couldn't keep the snarl of envy out of my voice.

"When I got up here tonight, he was crying himself to sleep. He thought—after what you said to him about how did he do it—he thought you knew."

"Knew what?"

"The truth about Sam. Jackie Slater kept on saying it right after they were divorced, but he was sure nobody would believe her."

"What truth?" I almost shouted.

"He's impotent," she said simply.

"Sam?" I stared at her stupidly for a few seconds. "It doesn't make any sense! Why the hell did he want to marry Linda Galen?"

"He liked her." There was a bleak look in her gray-green eyes. 'She liked him, and the thought of a comfortable relationship without sex appealed to her. Sex was never important in Linda's life, you know. It

123

wasn't during her first marriage with Sam, and she never intended her relationship with Andrea Marco to develop the way it did, but Andrea was a very dominant personality. Poor Linda!" She shook her head slowly. "That story of Sam raping her when he broke into her apartment was all a product of Andrea's vivid imagination."

"You still feel the same way about him, even though he was going to remarry Linda?" I asked.

Her face softened. "It was for my sake, really. He thought it wasn't fair to keep me tied to him, and he wouldn't listen when I told him I never wanted anything more. That's Sam! Always dredging up a new guilt complex!"

Sorel muttered something in his sleep, then turned his head and wedged it more firmly against the deep swell of her breasts. There was a faint smile on his face and, somehow, most of the wrinkles seemed to have disappeared from the usually puckered skin. Sonia smiled indulgently as she bent her head, then softly stroked his cheek with her hand.

"Sam!" She said his name with all the fondness of Mother Earth rampant. "He's my baby, and for keeps now!"

I walked over to the top of the bed, gripped the tiny copper bell between my thumb and index finger, then jerked it savagely from her earlobe. She looked up with a startled expression on her face as I moved away.

"What did you do that for, Rick?"

"I want a keepsake to remind me of the woman who could have been the most wonderful experience in my whole life, only she preferred to stay a mother," I told her. "Good-bye, Sonia."

"Sam will call you in the morning, Rick. He'll never forget what you've done for him tonight!"

"Tell him just to send money," I snarled. "If there's anything I hate, it's a two-bit comic with an infantile regression!"

I went back down the stairs and straight out of the house to the car in a kind of futile rage. It was two blocks away before my mind started to function again. "So you're crying?" it sneered inside my head. "Over some dame with a mother complex? When the night's still young, and you've got a choice between which one of two gorgeous broads you'll spend the rest of it with?"

Right then I nearly ran off the road. I had forgotten —how the hell could I ever do that?—that both Beverly and Jackie would be anxiously waiting to hear whether or not they were safe from the threat of Hugill. All I had to do was walk in, do the modest hero bit, and then have it made. I checked my watch quickly. It was still only a few minutes after midnight. There are times, I figured generously, when a mind that reminds you is a definite asset.

There was only one problem left, and that was to choose which gorgeous broad it should be. Jackie—the silver-blonde with the incredible figure; that symphony of bountiful spheres and harmonizing hollows! But then I also remembered she was about as solid between the ears, and her one-syllable conversation would drive anybody out of their minds if they had to listen to it for any length of time.

The redheaded Beverly, with that sharp, intelligent mind and strong sense of humor! I smiled fondly as I remembered her. The sharp planes of her attractive face, her tall slenderness. So maybe she was a little on the lean side, but what the hell did that matter? And a conversation with her would be bright and witty; something a guy could enjoy. It was just no contest, I decided, and pointed the car toward the high-rise building where she lived.

Beverly! I said her name over to myself, happily remembering it was all those intriguing exercises that kept her body lithe and taut. And she was a genuine redhead! My mind glazed for a moment at the thought. That last kiss she'd given me just before I left her apartment earlier. "Just an expression of feeling, you understand?" That was what she said, and she almost blushed when she said it. A great girl, Beverly. An intelligent, attractive, tremendously sincere girl, and it was a shame her first marriage hadn't worked out. How could she have been fooled by a creep like Hugill? She'd even been hoping he would marry her; I remembered her telling me that. Anyway, I idly thought, it just goes to prove she's a girl who won't be satisfied with anything less than marriage, from the moment she's sure the guy has fallen for her, and she for him.

Marriage! The full import of what I had just been thinking suddenly exploded inside my head. I shuddered convulsively, made a quick U-turn and headed back toward Beverly Hills, the sweat running cold down my face. Beverly could read all about it in the newspapers!

Ten minutes later I unlocked the front door and walked into my little status-symbol home. Jackie! I thought blissfully of all those bounteous spheres and delicious hollows as I switched on the light in the front hall.

"You can quit worrying right now, honey," I called out happily. "I fixed Hugill, but good! He'll never worry you anymore and—" I stopped right there. The living room was in darkness. So maybe she'd gone to sleep while she was waiting for her hero to return triumphant? The silver-blonde honey probably wanted to rest up her motor so it could run at full revs when I got back! I switched on the living room lights and the blissful smile slowly faded from my face as I realized the room was empty. That lousy, loud-mouthed starlet! I thought dismally. Chickened out on me and probably gone home to Harv!

I went over to the bar, made myself a king-sized drink, and then the razor-sharp Holman started figuring again. I was no slouch at verbal jousting, I told myself. So what if she did hint at marriage? I could neatly sidestep—pretend I never heard what she said—make like I had amnesia if things got real rough! I downed the drink in three convulsive gulps, then headed toward the phone. Genuine redhead, I chuckled as I dialed her number, you don't know it, but this is your lucky night!

"Yes?" A deep voice growled in my ear a couple of seconds later.

I took the phone away from my ear and stared at it for a moment, then decided the whole thing was just a freak of the telephone company. "Beverly?" I said hopefully into the mouthpiece.

"No," the deep voice said coldly. "This is Professor Urquehart. I'm afraid it's impossible for Miss Quillen to come to the phone right now. She's engaged in a somewhat unique experiment."

"Psychological?" I muttered.

"More physical then mental." The voice hardened. "And I might add, your call came at a goddamned inconvenient moment! Don't call again before ten in the morning!"

There was a sharp click as the bastard hung up on me. I walked morosely back to the bar and made myself another king-sized drink. Then I toasted the abysmal failure of their unique experiment, but there was no fun in it. The hell with it! I figured I might as well go to sleep rather than stand around with my frustrated thoughts. I took the drink for company, and headed for my bedroom.

I switched on the light, went over to the bureau, and put the drink down on top of it. The chair was cluttered with discarded clothes, which I swept onto the floor impatiently before I sat down. Since when, I wondered vaguely, had I been wearing a patterned silk blouse and a pair of canary-yellow pants? Then the glorious realization hit, and I leapt out of the chair and bounded to the side of the bed. I stripped the covers off with a sharp yank of my hand, then lost my breath.

Jackie opened her eyes, blinked a couple of times, then smiled sleepily. She was dressed for the heat, just wearing those briefest briefs, consisting of the two polka-dotted silk panels held together by thin silken strips across either side of her swelling hips. Her gorgeous coral-tipped twin spheres rose together in magnificent harmony as she took a long deep breath.

"Rick, honey," she murmured. "I thought you'd never get back!"

The hell with redheaded psychology majors! I thought happily as I gathered her into my arms. Who could tell? Maybe I was about to make love with a genuine silver-blonde!

More Mystery and Suspense Fiction from SIGNET

☐ **THE MEPHISTO WALTZ by Fred Mustard Stewart.** A masterpiece in suspense and quiet (the most deadly) horror. Only the strongest will resist its subtly diabolic power. (#Q4643—95¢)

☐ **HAIL, HAIL, THE GANG'S ALL HERE! by Ed McBain.** In this 87th Precinct mystery all of Ed McBain's detectives come together for the first time and they're all kept hopping. Some of the stories are violent, some touching, some ironic, but all are marked by the masterful McBain touch ... the "gang" has never been better. (#T5063—75¢)

☐ **FUZZ by Ed McBain.** An 87th Precinct Mystery which involves a homemade bomb, a couple of fun-loving youngsters and an ingenious extortion scheme which add up to big excitement. (#T5151—75¢)

☐ **THE ABORTIONIST by Martin Winslow.** Everyone knew about the young gynecologist—the police looked the other way, and fellow physicians sent him cases they didn't dare handle. Until that day he was arrested and put on trial. Then an entire town learned more about the abortionist and themselves than they cared to know. (#Q4265—75¢)

THE NEW AMERICAN LIBRARY, INC.,
P.O. Box 999, Bergenfield, New Jersey 07621

Please send me the SIGNET BOOKS I have checked above. I am enclosing $_____(check or money order—no currency or C.O.D.'s). Please include the list price plus 15¢ a copy to cover handling and mailing costs. (Prices and numbers are subject to change without notice.)

Name_____

Address_____

City_____ State_____ Zip Code_____

Allow at least 3 weeks for delivery